THE RINGER

TONY BLACK

Copyright © 2014 Tony Black

All rights reserved.

ISBN-13: 978-1500444921

ISBN: 1500444928

TONY BLACK

Tony Black has asserted his right to be identified as the author of this work under the Copyright, Designs and Patents Act 1988.

This book is sold subject to the condition that it shall not, by way of trade or otherwise, be hired, resold, lent out, or in any way circulated without the publisher's prior consent in any form of binding, cover or electronic format other than that in which it is published and without a similar condition, including this condition, being imposed on any subsequent purchaser.

First published in Scotland in 2014 by Pusher Press.

All similarities to actual characters — living or dead — are purely coincidental.

Cover image: Jim Divine

www.tonyblack.net

Reviews for Tony Black

"Tony Black is one of those excellent perpetrators of Scottish noir ... a compelling and convincing portrayer of raw emotions in a vicious milieu."

- *The Times*

"If you're a fan of the Ian Rankin, Denise Mina and Irvine Welsh this is most certainly one for you."

- *The Scotsman*

"Black renders his nicotine-stained domain in a hardboiled slang that fizzles with vicious verisimilitude."

- *The Guardian*

"Ripping, gutsy prose and a witty wreck of a protagonist makes this another exceptionally compelling, bright and even original thriller."

-*The Mirror*

"This up-and-coming crime writer isn't portraying the Edinburgh in the Visit Scotland tourism ads."

- The Sun

"Comparisons with Rebus will be obvious. But that would be too easy ... Black has put his defiant, kick-ass stamp on his leading man, creating a character that deftly carries the story through every razor-sharp twist and harrowing turn."

- Daily Record

"An authentic yet unique voice, Tony Black shows why he is leading the pack in British crime fiction today. Atmospherically driven, the taut and sparse prose is as near to the bone you are ever likely to encounter in crime noir. Powerful."

- New York Journal of Books

TONY BLACK

THE RINGER

TONY BLACK

Ah, my aching head.

The hell is that? Christ, something not right here.

I push myself up from the floor. That's when I smell the piss. No, tell me I've not pissed myself. The palms of my hands slip as I raise myself up. I slide back down, let my head settle a wee bit. Something definitely not right here. No, sir. Fucking sure it's not.

'Stauner, y'prick ...' I hear the words, but there's no one there. 'Aye, you, y'daft bastard.' It's Tambo, would know that voice anywhere.

Tambo, the fuck's he doing here? Haven't seen him outside the Boneyard. And if I'm anywhere near the Boneyard, I'm a dead man.

'Aye, Stauner, you're not wrong. Tambo here – I'd

pay for front-row seats to see this.' He claps hands. The noise rattles off the ceiling and the walls. I look around, just to make sure, to make certain, like ... but there's no one else there.

'Eh?' I go. 'The fuck's going on?'

My heart rate ramps. My lips are dry, my mouth feels like the bottom of a parrot's cage, as my Old Boy would say. My head hurts like someone's been at me with a hammer. Claw-end, likely.

I feel my hands sliding as I go to push myself up again. My arse is wet, soaking. There's a sting in my ring like I've just dropped some serious rocks. Fucking hope that's what it is, that or I've had the arsehole rode off me by some big-time buftie boy. A pro, likely.

'Jesus, man ...' I look down; it's blood.

'No, *fucking* hell ...' I don't know what to do. I'm lying in a pool of blood. There's piss and something else. I can't bear to say it ...

'No, y'bastards ... no fucking way. No, *why*?'

I lift my arm, slip.

I feel a *whoosh* at my back as I go over, then my head cracks off the floor.

The boards are cold, slippy.

I feel lost.

Out of it.

I bring a hand up to rub my stinging head – hurts like a pure bastard now, so it does. That's when I get the shock of my life.

'This can't be happening ...'

'Oh, aye, it is, Stauner ... fucking sure it is.' It's Tambo again. Where is the cunt, though?

'Tambo?' I go, 'That you? ... Well fucking show yourself ...'

I'm still rubbing my head, frantic like.

Can't take it in. I'm pure scoobied.

Some bastard's shaved my head. I know that

much. There's hair everywhere, on me, on the floor. *My* hair, but the lassies love my hair.

What's going on?

'Hello ... help me!'

As I call out, I hear laughter.

'Tambo, that you? The fuck's up? What have I done to you, man?'

More laughs.

Mad laughs, like the films and that.

Then a door slamming.

Through the darkness I hear something.

Footsteps.

Slow, at first.

Then faster ...

*****

Have to hand it to myself, got some sway with the lay-dees. See me, I'm one of those blokes that can pull any lassie they like. Put me in a room with say, five or ten lassies and they'd all be clocking me. Checking the package out and that. If I went off for a pish, they'd all be talking about me. They'd all be saying that's some fucking bit of raw meat there. Big Stauner's the man, alright. Wouldn't mind a piece of that. He looks a handy man ... wonder if he'd take a look at my plumbing? *Hahahahaha ...*

See, I've heard it ... they call me the Stauner cos I gets them frothing at the gash, likes. That's not me being big-headed. No danger. Just stating the facts of life. Some guys couldn't pull a hoor in a knockshop with tenners taped to their boaby. Me, I beat them off with a shitty stick. Known for it. Like I say, facts of life, likes.

Take this wee French lassie, for instance, doing the bar down at the Boneyard – Davie Geddes's club. I strolls up and gets a bevy, gets chatting. Hits it with the old, 'get yourself a wee something as well, love' ... I put a smile on it and the Frenchie's about ready to melt. Turns a real beamer on, could fry an egg on its forehead so you could.

'Thank you very much. It is really kind of you,' it goes.

'No worries,' I goes. 'Pure dead generous, me.' I does another wee smile there and before you know it the Frenchie's touching the hair, turning it behind the ear and all that. Now see me, I know what that means, like. Says the lassie's after it, wants it. Another bloke, he'd be clueless ... Wouldn't know about the old psychology and that. Not me. I'm on the ball. See, a lassie touching its hair is like a message. It's saying, I'm ready, willing and able to take you on. It's like dogs in the street, no difference. We're all pure animals at the best of times.

'So, you're not from around here,' I goes. Just starting up the chat, likes. Y'know, got to keep it general at first. Doesn't pay to go stomping in there and putting your cards on the table right away. They hate that, lassies. It's all about playing the game the way they want to play it, so it is.

'No, I am from Marseilles.'

'Alright, I thought you were French, likes.'

It smiles, got pure big brown eyes, so it has. 'Yes, I am French.'

Now see, your average Weegie lassie will give you a hard time at this stage – unless you're showing the green about, then it'll be on you like a fucking dog eating chips – but this Frenchie's cool as can be. I mean, it's into me big time, I can tell – it's a lassie after all – but it was making it pure plain that it had a wee bit more interest among the rank and file. Like they'd mess with the Stauner, though. The daft bastards.

I amps it up. Well, it's like an extra bit of interest for me. Pulling a lassie that every other cunt is after is what it's really all about. That's you getting a double top, so it is. 'So, what brings you down to the Boneyard?'

'I am travelling. I looked for work and found they were hiring.'

'Travelling, eh?'

That smile again; a fair rack on it, too. Something

about this lassie, I'm thinking – oh, aye, it's got a fanny. Good enough for me.

'Yes, I am ... how do you say, backpacking?'

'With friends?'

'No, I was with my boyfriend ... but we split up.'

See, that's what I'm talking about. Some daft prick's pulled this big French bit and fucked it up for himself. You get a nice bit of gear like that and you have to watch out. I know these things, but your average Joe is in the fucking dark. Blind, likes. I mean, it's horses for courses. You wouldn't send a guy with a face like Wayne Rooney after a lassie like this; he'd pure get his arse caned. Be embarrassing for the boy.

Not me, but.

Uh-huh.

I'm just the man for this action.

Known for it.

I'm chatting away to it and I can already hear the

bedsprings going, y'know, and it's got that face on. Moaning it is, pure fucking loving it. They all do, that's another thing, they all fucking love it, just don't like to admit it to themselves. Sure way to blow your chances is to make out that's what you're after, but ... a lassie thinks you're going for your hole and you're sent packing. Their terms, man. Their terms, that's the golden rule.

'That's a fucking shame,' I goes. 'I'm pure sorry to hear that.'

It shrugs, picks up a glass and starts wiping it with a wee bar towel.

Now, I can tell it's not into talking about this big break-up – fucking probably the love of its life and all that – but I also know it's kicked the fucking door open for Big Stauner to walk right through. One of the sure and certainties that: a lassie on the rebound. You get them when they're a wee bit fucked up in the head and you're onto a winner. Want to start rubbing my hands together, so I do.

'Well, look, it can't be easy for a lassie in a new toon, especially after what you've just been through.'

It loves that wee bit on the end there, near puts a tear in its eye, fucking class, that's me, class; no one's got my moves. '... so, let me give you my number and if you need someone to go for a coffee or a wee trip to the pictures or that, just you give me a jingle, eh?'

It nods, puts down the towel and the glass, and then it's tearing off a wee bit of the till receipt and handing me a pen. I write down my number and give it a wee smile, one of they sidey-ways ones that kinda looks innocent enough but, the likes of me know, can also say you're getting rode, doll. Sure and fucking certain you are. Might not be tonight, might not be tomorrow night, but Big Stauner has staked his claim and now it's just a matter of time.

Got to hand it to the Boneyard, pulled some gash in here. Thing is, but, wee Davie Geddes – he's the owner of the joint – has a problem with the bold Stauner. Just one of them things. Thinks my face doesn't fit. I'm not saying he's out of order, no way, I wouldn't be putting any aspersions out about wee Davie, him being such a Big Man and all that. He's known about the town. A kent face, like they say. Had a rep as a razor man back in the day – when his wee man complex was in full force. Apparently he enjoyed the carving so much that he still does the Christmas turkey with a cut-throat. There's hardly a slashed coupon comes out his club that Davie hasn't administered personally. So I'm careful ... careful as a priest pouring his communion wine doon the neck of a choir boy.

'Got any jellies, Stauner?'

It's some wee ned I don't even know, but he knows my handle.

'Jellies ... aye, how many you after?'

I does the deal, slips the green in the sky rocket and the ned slopes off, Adidas trackies rustling. As I watch him go I'm thinking about wee Bri, the boy I used to have carrying the stash. See, that's the way to do it: one boy on the stash, one boy on the cash. Pigs can't do you for dealing then. But wee Bri was a greedy cunt; twenty sheets a night I started paying him and there he was last week asking for doublers. Fuck that. Wee radge can go swivel. If I see him about here dealing, though, he'll be hanging from his swingers. Fucking sure he will.

I'm two paces behind the wee ned I've just offloaded some of my finest jellies on when there's a slap on my shoulder, then there's a grab at my waistband and I'm hoiked backwards.

'The fuck's going on here?' I goes.

I'm spun around, turn to see Tambo — a big beefy biffer in a black leather. He's got a shaved head and a stack of wee star tats to complete the look. They call him Tambo because he's Glasgow's answer to Rambo, given his hair-lip and love of steroids.

'Up them stairs,' he goes.

'*Y-wha*?' I know what's up the stairs. 'Got to be joking me.'

The big lad leans over, juts his jaw. I can see the bottom row of his teeth, all grey and broken. Fucking strangers to Colgate. He's near enough growling at me now — fair puts the shits up you, let me tell you. The Stauner's a lover not a fighter, likes.

'Don't make me tell you again, y'cunt!' goes Tambo.

I look him up and down, playing up a wee bit, I know, but you've got to stand your ground with these radges or they tear you a new arsehole for the fun of it. The facts of life, likes.

'Aye alright, keep your fucking hair on!' Soon as I say this I regret it, y'know that way, when you've done something that's going to have some ramifications you don't want. Happens to me all the time, so it does.

'Cheeky cunt!' He lamps me. One big double-decker, puts me on the floor. I can hear the wee canaries singing round the top of my head. In no time there's two more biffers, both baldy boys in black leathers, leaning over me. I think I'm seeing double but then they grab my arms, yank me up, and ram me head-first for the door.

'Take him up to Davie,' goes Tambo.

There's a bang, then a shriek of hinges and I'm on the stairs.

I'm thinking, this is a pure brasser. No the scene for the Stauner. No by a long stroke.

If anyone sees me getting paraded through the Boneyard by this pair of shit-kickers it'll look like I'm for a doing. Then I remember that I probably am.

'Look, the fuck is this all about?' I goes, trying to cool the beans right down.

Laughs.

The pair of them start choking on that.

Thing is I know fine well what it's all about, fucking sure I do. But that only makes it all the worse.

At the top of the stairs is a door. Biffer #1 gives it a whack and a wee Judas hole slides open. I see two watery-green eyes. What my Old Boy would say were two piss-holes in the snow. I know who they belong to, but in case there's any doubts, Davie Geddes shouts, 'This fucker again!' He slams the slot and a second later the keys are turning in the lock. 'Get the cunt inside!'

There's two wee lassies — schoolies likely — over in the corner, silvery dresses and St Tropez tans. Nice gear, has to be said. Nothing I'd be chucking out of bed for farting that's for sure. Even if it was fifty-fifty you'd get hair on it. I mean, could they be eighteen? Fucking never. I looks them over and I'm getting the glad-eye, fucking sure I am. I'm grinning my head off and then there's a clatter at the rear of me and I realise I've been hit. Rabbit-punched.

I drop harder than the first shite after a night on the stout.

'Fucking hell ... that's out of order,' I goes. I'm on the deck, rolling over, thinking the bastard's coming for me again. Then I realise it was just a sample. A wee taster.

'Sort yourself out, arsehole.' Davie's buttoning up his shirt as he stares down at me. 'On your feet ...' he looks over at the schoolies, grabs biffer #2's arm, points, 'and get that pair of tarts out of here!'

In no time the room's been cleared. Davie's put his tackle away and stands in front of me, running fingers through his greasy hair. He's twitching a bit, rubbing his nose. Could do with a wee line of Charlie, I'm thinking; it's half on my mind to make him an offer for a wee baggie, but then I remember that's the reason I'm in here and maybe it'll not go down too well.

Davie points again, at me this time. 'Are you away with the bloody pixies, son?' There's froth on the sides of his mouth when he's finished. No shit, there is.

'Eh?' I goes.

He struts, puts his hands on his hips, halts. 'I thought I told you about dealing in my club already.'

I see he's off the dial, so I tries a big smile but I remember he's not a lassie and that'll get me nowhere. 'Eh now, Davie, to be fair mate you never said I couldn't ...'

He looks at the biffers, #1 and #2; they shrug together.

'What are you fucking on about, laddie?' goes Davie.

I feel my head tip to the side, always does that — kinda like a jolt or what have you — when I'm nervous. I'm — what's the phrase? — lunging or reaching or something. Just trying to dig myself out this massive hole I'm in. 'Y'see, Davie, man, what you said to me was ... don't let me *catch you* dealing in the club again.'

He touches the corners of his mouth, tilts his head to the same angle as mine. He looks well scoobied. I watch him for a minute, then he folds his arms, straightens himself and turns to the biffers again. 'He for real?'

There's laughter.

I can hear their jewellery rattling.

I straighten my head, 'Now, Davie, fair's fair ... I did my best not to let you catch me dealing in your club, but is it my fault, really, that you run such a tight ship that it's an impossibility?' I'm on a loser. I can tell. They're laughing me up more than ever, but I keep going. I mean, what fucking choice do I have, eh? 'I see that was a mistake now, Davie, I mean I see what I really should have done was keep the dealing out the club ... well away, like.'

Davie and the biffers are huddled, laughing their ends off.

I change tactics, try to keep it zipped. Seems the best policy in the circumstances. Still, surprised he never went for the flattery angle. Usually works a treat for me, that does.

There's the sound of throats being cleared.

A cough.

Some wheezing.

'Turn this cunt up,' goes Davie.

The big lads head for me. I'm smacked in the belly and fold like a Swiss Army knife. I think I'm going to puke my guts up, but before I can I'm lifted by my heels and my pockets are rifled. Everything's falling round my ears as the pair of big fuckers shake me about, occasionally banging my head off the floor for a laugh.

'Aye okay ... okay ... enough's enough. I'd have tipped my pockets if you'd asked.'

Davie Geddes stands before me. I'm staring at his Red or Dead shoes – they go for about a ton in Schuh – as he stands there watching the wee wraps and bigger baggies falling on the floor. He delves for a wrap of fast powder, picks it up and shoves it in my coupon. Pretty hard, it has to be said. I'm thinking this is all a bit unnecessary and not how I'd be handling this situation, not at all.

'See this ... this is what I'm fucking talking about!' goes Davie. He's holding the powder under my nose.

'Aye, Davie, lesson's learned man, and all that. Lesson's learned, mate,' I goes.

He steps back. I see him shaking his head at me as he turns and walks to his desk to cut himself a few lines, at my expense. 'Get this cunt out my face!' he goes.

'Yes, Boss,' goes biffer #1.

I'm turned over again, grabbed by the scruff of the neck and marched towards the door.

I'm thinking of something to say, trying to form the words, but my mouth's pure dried over, so it has, as I watch my bit of posh being sliced up.

Davie speaks up, 'Oh, and make sure he learns his

lesson this time ... there won't be a next time for the stupid wee cunt. Bastarding sure there won't!'

*****

There's no way this is happening, no fucking way.

I feel a tightening round my neck. Like a noose.

'Fuck off, go away ...'

There's three of them, Jonesy at the front, but he's just telling the other two what to do. They're bigger than him, older.

'No, fuck off ... I didn't do it!' It's all I can think to say. I'm still a kid, *Christ*. I am, you can't do this to a kid. You can't.

'She was only fourteen!' he goes.

I'm kicking out, trying to fend them off. But they're too big. They grab my arms. I feel their fingers clamp me still.

'I didn't do it!'

'You're a liar,' shouts Jonesy. 'Get his pants down.'

Jonesy has a stick, a cricket stump. He whacks me on the bare thighs as the other two wrestle my jeans past my knees. I feel trapped. They have my arms. My legs are tied, wrapped up in my jeans and pants.

'You're getting it now, y'dirty wee bastard!' goes Jonesy.

'I didn't do anything ... I *didn't* ... I – I – I ...'

I get another whack with the stick, in the mouth this time. I can feel the sting of it. My teeth scream out in pain, there's blood. It tastes like the time I bit my tongue when I came off my bike outside the Co-Op.

Lots of blood.

Salty, and strange.

I see it drip from my mouth as they turn me over.

My face is pushed in the dirt.

I feel a foot on my back.

I taste the ground, can hardly breathe as Jonesy roars.

'You're getting it now!'

In a second I feel like a knife has went inside me. A hot burning knife, tearing at my insides.

Jonesy's still roaring: 'This what it was like, eh ... Was it? ... Was it?'

I try to scream, but can't.

Why?

Why can't I scream?

My breathing quickens.

I'm only sixteen, string-bean they call me, they're grown men. I can't fight them off. Jonesy shouts at them, but I can't hear what he says anymore ... I'm all pain, nothing but pain inside me.

A bell sounds.

Suddenly, I'm awake.

I'm panting heavily.

Drenched in sweat.

The duvet is wrapped around my neck.

I struggle to re-enter the real world.

Panic and relief jostle in me.

Is it over?

I slap my head with the heel of my hand. Turn to face the ringing phone beside my bed. I pick it up, but my heart is still pounding, my breath heavy.

It's the French lassie, *Monique* it calls itself.

I gasp, 'Ho, result, Stauner man ...'

The phone's still going, so's my ticker. Bad shit that. Nightmares. Been having that one for years.

'Hello, Stauner here.' I plays up to the lassie, I mean, can't look too keen, eh.

'Oh, hello too, it is Monique ... do you remember?'

Do I remember? Fucksake. Was only last night; mind you, doesn't do to let it think I *do* remember. Uh-uh. Got to keep them guessing, 'Who's this?' I go.

There's a gap on the line.

Then, 'From the club, the Boneyard ...'

I acts stupid. 'Oh, aye, aye ...' It's all about the tone in the voice, likes. Let it think I'm scoobied, don't know it from Adam, keeps it on edge and all that.

Another gap.

'So, erm, I thought I would call,' goes Monique, '... just to see if you were really meaning what you said.'

Now I'm thinking this lassie's at it. Playing me at my own game, eh? I mean I was fucking rubber, as per, and there was some chemicals taken, too. I could have said fucking anything to it. I stalls, then plays a dummy the late great Davie Cooper would have been proud of. 'What I said ... oh, aye, aye ... *that*.'

It giggles. It's a pure turn on that, has to be said. Don't know why, French lassies, eh.

'Well, how would you like to meet me for, erm, a coffee?'

'Coffee?' Be some expensive poncy job, no served up with a wink and a tab after a night in the sack, which is what I'm after. Still, remember the rules here, Stauner boy. 'Aye, coffee would be just the job.'

'Good. That's great. Can we meet at one ... in Starbucks on the High Street?'

Fucking star-fucks is what I'm after. 'Aye, go on. See you there at one, doll.'

'Okay.' It giggles again. 'I'll see you there.'

The line dies.

I give a wee nod to the phone. Bit of a result there, Stauner Boy. One for coffee, two for cream! Heh-heh. Well, even by my standards that would be some going, but got to look ahead. The facts of life, likes.

I ease myself out of bed. The old ribs give me a turn. Quite a doing I got off Geddes's biffers last night. I touch the side of my ribcage ... *argh* ... pure fucking agony, so it is. I straighten my back to try and push the pain away but it just shifts round there like some pikey shown the road.

Taken a few good boots to the kidneys, too.

Fucking bastards.

I push myself onto my feet. That's when I feel the head spinning. I take a deck in the mirror and see there's some bruising around my jaw; there'll be a nice shiner on the way as well, likes as not.

I grip the bridge of my nose, tweak. It's sore, sore as outdoor buggery so it is, but I don't think it's broken.

'What a fucking doing.'

What a bunch of cunts, and that Davie Geddes, what a scripto bastard. 'They'll get theirs,' I goes. 'Fucking sure they will ... even if it kills me.'

Turning me out last night cost me the best part of 500-bar ... how am I supposed to make that back, eh?

That's the thing with these big hot-shots like Davie Geddes: they forget where they came from. And where was that? Same as me, same as the punters paying twenty sheets a night to get into his club and fuck knows how much more to get themselves tanked-up on his watered-doon bevy.

Aye, he's a big man now, but I mind him when he had holes in his gutties, as my Old Boy would say. Not wrong about much, my Old Boy. Folk took the pish out him, and in the end even the doctors had to take the pish out him — with a rubber tube likes — but my Old Boy wasn't wrong about much.

'Davie Geddes's going to get his, fucking sure he is,' I blast away. I try to take a swing at the wall but my ribs scream out in agony.

I'm hunched over, leaning on the wall, as the mobi buzzes again. A text this time.

SEE YOU AT ONE, DO NOT FORGET! M XX

Christ, it's keen.

Maybe get the boaby today after all.

I have a wee smile to myself and decide it's time to get rocking and rolling. Be the Lynx for this chick, proper stuff, not the cheapo Poundies copy.

I run a shower, hot as I can manage, and climb in. For the first few seconds I'm recoiling in pain, just pure scrunching up my face at the agony of it all.

I can see a few more bruises on the sides of my legs and round my wrists where biffer #1 grabbed me as #2 booted the shit out me. There's all kinds of scrapes and cuts on my knees. That's from where I landed. I remember landing a few times cos the bastards kept picking me up to add to their earlier damage.

'The pricks.'

I turn my back to the jets coming from the shower and look at my hands, there's red streaks down the palms. I wince when I remember putting out my hands to break my fall and the tarmac taking layers of skin off. Like razor blades, so it was.

I tuck my hands under my arms and try to let the warm water massage some of the pain away.

'Aye, nice try, son.'

Not happening.

I give the shower the best part of ten minutes and then I'm back through in the bedroom, curled up and shivering. I know I've got to get moving. Got to get down the town and grab a hold of this French lassie. I know the only way I'm moving is with a hit on the fast powder, so I'm out the bed again and rifling my pockets for a wrap.

Fuck all.

That's when I remember Davie Geddes poking his scrawny beak in my supply.

'The bastard!'

I'm cursing and cursing.

'The bastard's pure robbed me!'

There's a sudden bolt of energy runs through me and before I know it I'm lashing ten bells out the mattress with my fists. I don't care about the ache in my ribs anymore. I'm way beyond that.

'Davie, you bastard ...   I'm having you ... Fucking

right I am ...'

I keep the frenzy up for a few minutes before I collapse in a cowp on the bed.

I'm pure shagged.

As I lay there fuming, it dawns on me I've been battering ten bells out the mattress for nothing. I'd be better sucking it up, just writing off all last night's antics. I know there's no way I'll be getting my own back on Davie Geddes. I'd be better writing off the stash, and the sore ribs, and the pure embarrassment of it all.

That's what I'm thinking as I lie there: it's all just a pure brasser for the Stauner.

*****

I puts the finishing touches to the hair, been best part of forty-five minutes at it, but has to be done if you're the Stauner, mind you. The facts of life, likes. I've got the back and sides blow-dried all wavy and the top's sitting there like some surfer's just about to appear on his board. The way I like it. I runs a bit of the Dax putty through, adding a nice finishing touch, and steps back from the mirror. I have to congratulate myself, it's not everyone has a head of hair like that.

'That's the game, Stauner,' I goes. 'Have that Monique lassie frothing at forty paces.'

I smiles to myself when I think of the likes of that fat-tongued cook off the telly. Fucking Jamie whatever. I mean, he might be alright at making sure the bairns get their five portions a day and all that, but what chance has he of giving some lassie a portion with hair like that? Cunt needs a word with himself about his barnet. I shake the head, dismissively likes, when I think about how much of an unstoppable sex machine the Stauner would be with his coupon on the telly every day.

'They'd be queued round the block, like some Harry Potter film was on.' I has a wee think about what I've just said and realise the queue would be full of bairns and that wouldn't do for the Stauner at all. Sure it wouldn't. No way, José. No' after that incident with the Old Boy; one member of the family being cried a stoat-the-ball is enough.

'No. No.' I bite down hard. I don't want to go there, don't want to think about those days. 'The wee bitch asked for it. The fucking wee cockteaser.'

I turns from the mirror and goes over to the dresser on the other side of the bed-sitter. Hardly room to swing a cat in here, I'm thinking. Would like a bit more space, but with the bastard Geddes robbing me the chances of moving onward and upward for the bold Stauner are limited.

I'm feeling a bit jaded, a bit crabbit, as I lift the Lynx off the dresser and direct it towards my armpit.

'Oh, Christ.'

It's empty.

I look about for another tin, but there's nothing else here except for the Blue Stratos that was left in the bag the hospital gave me when my Old Boy died.

'Aw, fucksake.'

Needs must. I rattle off the top and splash a bit of the Blue Stratos. It's strong enough, but I'm surprised to see it's not actually blue. Must be the bottle, I'm thinking as I start to button up my shirt and head out the door.

My mind's on the French lassie, not how I'm gonna play it. Uh-huh. There's no need for that kind of lark. Thinking about a lassie is the fastest road to a knockback. You never give them the space in your head. Once they're in there they call the shots. And there's no woman calls the shots with likes of me; I'm the top jockey and they need to know that from the off. Nah, what I'm thinking about is how long it'll take me to get this one on the job. Strategy – that's what it's all about. The facts of life, likes.

There's a bit of a scuffle on Jamaica Street, just across from MacSorley's drinker, between two dafties. Look like junkies, but I don't know the faces. I cross over and paint the smile on my coupon.

'Morning, boys.' I tip the wink, tap the side of my nose.

They turn to me, look scoobied.

I goes: 'Just saying, nice morning for it.' I let that hang, let them register my face and approachability –

they could be new to the neighbourhood and every one of those dafties is a potential customer. See, that's me, thinking ahead. Always thinking. And Christ alone knows I need to think of expanding the market after last night.

When I get to the Starbucks on Argyle Street, this Monique lassie is already in place, sitting in the window. It's got a big cup of coffee – must be a pint there – in front of it. The table wobbles a bit as it stands up to greet me.

'Alright, doll,' I goes.

Monique reaches over and plants a kiss on my cheek.

Aye, aye, I'm thinking.

And then it reaches round to my other cheek and plants another kiss there. Fucking result, Stauner, I'm telling myself.

I puts a hand up and takes a step back, I mean, doesn't pay to play into its hands. That's mistake number one right there: letting a lassie think you're into it. I'm putty in no lassie's hands, that's what the whole toon says. 'Think I'll just go and get a coffee, eh.'

I turns for the counter and it looks a wee bit scoobied, a bit subdued: just where I want it to be. At the counter I puts my order in, then turns around and winks back at Monique. That's enough to put a smile on the lassie's face. See, doesn't pay to play the hard hand too often, got to keep them sweet as well. Sweet, but on edge, that's how you keep the upper hand. A lassie should be constantly questioning itself, constantly wondering what it's doing right and wrong, or the controlling hand starts to slip.

Still. This one's a wee brammer, so it is. I take a sketch at the legs, black stockings all the way up to what looks like sussie-tops peeking beneath the wee short skirt. What the losers down the Boneyard would call 'well worth forty wanks'. What I call a good notch; oh aye, I'll be having myself a good wee French roll before long.

I takes the coffee off the immigrant at the till and counts my change – got to be sure with that sort – and goes back to the French lassie. It doesn't get up this time, which gives me an eyeful of the wee baps it's got in one of those push-up bra things. I say wee, but I mean a good handful. That's the mistake a lot of losers make, eyeing the big jugglies. Wrong. A handful is enough. And some of those big-titted hoors get ideas about themselves; think they're up there with yon Jordan lassie. Wrong again.

'So, how you settling into Glasgow?' I goes, all Mr Friendly like.

It starts to nod, squints the big brown eyes to the side as if it's looking for the right words, and goes: 'Yes, I am well. Today, I don't work so that is always a good thing, I think.'

It smiles and I smile back. 'Aye, well, I wouldn't fancy working down the Boneyard … behind the bar, anyway.' I'm thinking about Geddes and his pugs from the night before again and I feel my blood surging.

'It can be hard, always a late night.'

It makes me laugh when it says this, but it's no idea why. 'Aye, aye.' I pick up my coffee. It's not that warm, tastes weak as well. I look back to the till and give a mean stare to the counter lassie. 'Could you not find a better job? ... It's a big toon.'

Monique crosses legs over and I get another sketch at those sussie tops. 'Well, I know this work from Marseilles and from Paris and Mr Geddes has been very kind to me.'

I'm thinking: I fucking bet he has. Dirty cunt. But go with, 'Aye, well, I'd watch that Davie Geddes.'

It says something in French, a word, sounds like 'quack' but then it corrects itself. 'I mean, why?'

'Well, let's just say oor Davie is a bit of a player.'

'A player you say ... I do not understand.'

I puts down my coffee mug, leans in. 'See when you're in the Boneyard, working and that, have you not noticed that Geddes is a wee bit dodgy?'

It shrugs. Kinda sexy and French, it has to be said. 'No, I think Mr Geddes is my friend. He is good to me, I think.'

'Oh, aye!' I let out a loud huff. 'Doll, he's likely

trying to get into your French knickers.'

It shakes its head. 'Oh, no. He is old enough to be my father.'

I look away, take a deck at a wee blonde piece that's wiping something white and frothy off its top lip. I'm thinking, I'd put something white and frothy there, darlin'. I goes: 'Old enough to be your father or not, all I'm saying is – watch him. Davie Geddes isn't to be trusted.'

'Oh, but I do trust him and he trusts me … look here.' It leans over to grab up a handbag, those perky baps jiggle, and I feel my eyes widen. 'Look …'

'Jesus Christ, is that what I think it is?'

It curls down the corners of its mouth. 'It is a money bag.' It opens the bag up, right in the middle of fucking Starbucks as well. 'Mr Geddes gave me this money to take to the bank.'

I quickly snatch the bag from Monique. It jumps a little but stays in its seat, big doe-eyes watching me as I delve inside and clock the best part of a grand in fivers and tenners. 'He gave you this? Just like that?'

'Yes. As I say, he trusts me.'

I'm thinking there's trust and there's trust. And I know Davie Geddes doesn't trust a fucking soul. There's a moment when I can't get my head around this, and then it suddenly slots into place. 'He's just trying to impress you, doll.'

'What?'

'He's showing off ... wants you to think he's the Big Man, that he's loaded, that he's got money to throw about.'

'But why me?' It looks as dippit as Marilyn Monroe when it was mailing in the dumb-bint act back in the black and white day.

'Why? ... Because he wants to ride you, darlin'!' It looks a bit scoobied, so I paint a wee smile on: 'The facts of life, likes.'

*****

I've just put the Pot Noodle down when there's a chap at the door. At first I get a wee bit pissed off, I mean, it's dinner time and all that, but then the knock comes again and it's a wee bit harder now.

Thud.

Thud.

Could be the pigs, I'm thinking. And then I realise that if it was the pigs they'd be battering down the door and make no mistake, tends to get a wee bit jumpy when there's Class-As concerned, does Mr Bacon.

I walks over to the door and I can hear voices. Sounds like a bloke and a lassie, but I can't make out a word they're saying. I'm tempted to lay low for now, cos I'm still not convinced a visit from Davie Geddes's pugs isn't on the cards, and then I take a sketch at the Pot Noodle and I realise I'm Hank Marvin and I want this situ sorted now.

'Who's that?' I bawls out.

The voices still. Then there's a bark. 'Eh, I'm looking for the boy that sells the eccies,' he goes.

I fling the door open and reach out to grab the

first body I find. It's some wee raver, a proper beat boy in the Kappa cap and baggie joggies. I grab his trackie top and yank him inside the door.

'What you playing at?' I goes.

His pal's crammed himself in behind him, another Cheesy Quaver with a face so covered in plooks it looks like he's been batted about the chops with a bag of hundreds and thousands. 'Whoa, whoa, cool the beans, Big Man!' he goes.

'Cool the beans?' I goes. 'What you fucking playing at broadcasting to the stair that I'm dealing?'

The pair of dafties look at each other, shrug. 'Sorry, mate,' goes the first one. 'So you got any gear?'

I leans out the door. There's an old giffer with the white candyfloss hair and the corned-beef legs from sitting too close to the fire watching the goings. I can see right into its wee flat, the sad, empty wee world that's only brightened by the Emmerdale tune going off in the background.

'You want a picture?' I goes.

It looks at me like I've asked it to take boaby up the lum and then scuttles back inside, slamming the door. I starts to laugh to myself as I hear it rattling the chain and turning the key in the lock.

'Daft old bint,' I goes.

I turn and head back to the bedsit and the two tripped-out roasters in Adidas. They're sniffling and shivering and I know already what it is they're after. A trick of the trade. The facts of life, likes.

'Downers, boys?'

They start nodding away, go: 'Aye, aye.'

I sort them out and take a few sheets off them. They seem happy enough so I show them the business end of my boot on the way out as a reminder. 'Now, I'm warning you ... don't be broadcasting my handle about this stair again. I don't want a knock from the pigs cos that old boot over the way's got it in for me.'

'Sorry big man, no offence or that, eh?'

I give them a nod; wee fannies just need told

who's boss. They swagger away, all chuffed as Leisure Suit Larry with their wee stash.

I settle back in, count the readies and pocket the lot. Hardly cause for celebration or worth tucking under the mattress, but after the incident at the Boneyard I know I need all the green I can get my hands on.

By the time I get to my dinner the Pot Noodle's gone cold.

'Fucksake!' I goes.

I'm reeking at the thought of pouring the lot down the sink because Pot Noodles don't grow on trees and the Stauner has more important things to be spending his hard-earned on. I shakes my head. 'Can't live on flogging downers to beat boys, man. Fucking sure you can't.'

I know a trip to the Boneyard's called for. I need to get cashed-up with some easy money flogging Harry Hills to the clubbers, but I know another visit to Davie Geddes's gaff will likely be my last.

'Bastard!'

I lashes out with the boot and knocks the coffee table over. The Pot Noodle goes flying, I'm fully scoobied as I watch it sort of hang in the air for a second like it's defying gravity, and then it lands on the carpet with a watery splash. A greasy layer of slop, noodles and sweetcorn covers a fair stretch of the already manky carpet now as I stand there fuming, just pure raging at the kip of the joint and my utter, utter nightmare of a situation.

'Fuck this. I mean just FUCK this right off.'

I know I can't afford to go out, but I need to find the space to think and the four walls of a manky bedsit isn't going to do. I grabs my Ben Sherman off the back of the door and heads out for a pint down the drinker.

As I'm locking up I hear the old bint's door creaking behind me again. I turns and catches it clocking me up and down like I'm some sort of criminal. It's seriously eyeballing me like I'm a nonce or that. I'm beyond speechless, but manage a few words cos this is the Stauner we're dealing with here.

'What the fuck do you want now?' I goes.

It closes the door a bit further but it's still there, looking at me like it knows something I don't. 'Are you fucking deaf?' I goes, turning, fronting up to it. 'I asked you a question.'

The door edges a little closer to the jamb, then it blurts in that pissy, whiney, croaky voice that old cunts have: 'I've called the police!'

'You wha–?' I moves forward a couple of quick paces, got the shoulders back and the chest out because I know it won't like that, but as I reach the other side of the stair, it's got the door closed and I get a waft of lavender in my coupon.

'What did you say about the police?' I starts thumping on the door but there's the sound of the chains going again and I know it thinks it's safe. 'You fucking old bitch!' I yells out. As I starts banging on the door I hear another door opening down the corridor and turns to see some Rick Moranis lookalike in his string vest and chewing-gum coloured Ys coming at me. He's got the glaiket look of the just-roused-from-sleep dole mole that I know he is.

'Get back in your hole, y'wee cunt!' I blasts. He

yelps a bit and turns tail.

As another door slams I'm stood there with my pulse racing and not a single thought entering my head.

'Shit. Shit. Shit,' I goes.

I know I'm a goner if I stay around because I've a couple of kilos of Moroccan Black and a good slab of Gold Leaf sitting in the bottom of the wardrobe. I heads back to my front door and starts to ferret in my breeks for the key to open back up.

'Come on, Stauner, keep the head ...'

I've just sprung the lock when I hear the police sirens blaring up Jamaica Street.

'No. Jesus-fucking-Christ!'

*****

I can almost smell the bacon sizzling as I bomb it down the stairs and out the close door. There's a definite whiff of pork in the air, with sirens and blue lights going at full tilt. The first instinct is to get a jig on and peg it for all I'm worth, but the Stauner knows better. I slips into MacSorley's and saunters up to the bar.

'Pint of McEwan's, mate.'

I gets a nod of approval from the new barman, not a face I know but he's obviously a good Rangers man and I like to see that. If he was a Tim I'd be watching for a gob in the pint; they've all had the arse rode off them by priests and not to be trusted. The facts of life, likes.

I'm downing the first gulp of my Mick Jagger, letting my heart rate return to a more settled pace, when I feels a wee tug on my shoulder. I'm thinking: 'Fuck me. Pig scum.' And then I hear a voice that sends a wee shiver through me.

'Hello, my friend.' It's Monique.

I wipes the froth off my chops, goes: 'What you doing here, doll?'

It smiles at me, tilts its head to the side. I'm trying to suss the look on its coupon, but my eyes are drawn down to the puppies that are pushing through the polo-neck sweater. The sweater's tight, black lambswool, by the looks of it, but it's wearing a red bra underneath and I can just about make out the sheen on the silk. Brammer, I'm thinking, and I feel a wee semi coming on.

'I was in the neighbourhood,' it goes. 'That's what you say, yes?'

I nods away, but gets distracted when The Proclaimers come on the speakers giving it laldy about a letter from America. The fucking wee Hibbie cunts — I mean when did they last see any silverware? A disgrace to Scottish football. And they play in green as well.

'Aye, just passing, were you?' I goes.

It nods away, and it's a fair nod, so it is, but the baps stay solid. 'Well, the truth is, I knew where you lived ...'

I lets a wee smile creep up my coupon. 'Oh aye, you been following me, eh?'

It starts to giggle. 'Maybe.'

I reaches out and plants a wee slap on its arse. 'You bad girl.'

It seems to like it, being French and all that. 'Ooh! I will have to be a bad girl more often, I can see.'

I tips the wink and as I turn to the barman I can see the good old Billy Boy is nodding in approval. 'One for the lady, mate?' he goes.

'Aye there'll be one for the lady, alright,' I goes, just loud enough for Monique to hear and that smile of hers widens out a bit. I orders up a wee half-pint, cos that's what I buy lassies. I'm no getting into this four pound for a bottle of green Bacardi or cocktails and that. No danger. If the Mick Jagger's good enough for the Stauner, it's good enough for any lassie. The facts of life, likes.

We takes a wee table and I'm glad when The Proclaimers go off, but then this crowd of old cunts in black trousers and black silky waistcoats appear at the front of the bar and start bringing out the trumpets and saxophones. Just the sight of them bursts my head; I mean, they should be locked away in some old giffer farm by now, surely.

'What's the matter?' it goes.

'Fucking old bastards setting up, there ...'

'It looks like some kind of band, jazz maybe.'

It smiles and I realise it's too stupid to know what it's saying; they're all the same. But with a rack on it like that, I suppose it doesn't really matter. I mean, I'm not putting it on Mastermind or that. Leave the thinking to the Stauner; that's the only thinking it needs to do.

'So, do you stay nearby then?' I goes.

'Quite near, yes. I have an apartment in Charing Cross.'

'Oh, aye, nice one.' It's a fair trek from the Cross, but it looks fit enough for it. Fit for a bit more, I'd say. 'So, you not working tonight, Sugartits?'

It smiles, starts to fiddle with the hair and I'm thinking: Oh, aye.

The eyelids flutter at me as it speaks, 'No, I have the *whole* night free.'

I'm only half listening and I have to do a double take cos I think it's just said its hole's free the night.

'What's that?'

'Mr Geddes has let me take the night off.'

The mention of that flash bastard gets my goat, big time. 'Still after you, then ...'

It giggles, slaps me. That's the thing with this type of lassie, no clue what it's packing there. Not a scoobie. 'He is too old for me.' It leans forward and starts to play with the collar of my shirt. 'I only like younger men.'

By this stage I know I'm well and truly in there and I'm well impressed with myself. Even by my standards it's been a quick wee quest. I've never pulled a Frenchie before, either, and I'm looking forward to finding out if it's true what they say about them being the best rides and all that. But softly, softly. Don't want it getting any ideas that it can get its hooks into me that easy; they get those hooks in and next you know it they've got their hands in your pocket.

I leans back a wee bit, puts it in its place. 'So what did you have to do for Davie to get the night off, then?'

The eyes narrow a bit, then: 'What do you mean?'

'I mean, doll, Davie Geddes doesn't do something for nothing ... there must've been something in it for him.'

It nods quickly, like the penny's just dropped in its wee head. 'Of course, yes.' It picks up the half-pint, takes a sip and winces a little. Tastes a bit sharp for it, but the lassie will get used to it. They all do. Lots of things they have to get used to the taste of. 'Yes, I have accepted a promotion from him today, so Mr Geddes said I were to lift a glass.' It raises the half-pint and smiles, a big wide beam of teeth shine out. As it does so I notice the blue lights flashing outside stop suddenly and there's the rumble of meat-wagons going back to the pig farm.

'Eh, promotion?' I goes.

'Yes, I'm the, how you say, chargehand now.'

I leans back in my chair and picks up my own pint;

top bevy it is as well, I'm thinking, as I quaff a good belt of it. There's a wee mouse on a wheel running about inside my skull as I take in what Monique's just told me and I can see a stack of possibilities coming down the Clyde.

'Chargehand, eh?'

'Yes. I am very happy.'

'So you're like in charge of ringing up the tills and that, at the end of the night, like?'

'Correct. I am having to concentrate all the time, but there is more money.'

I nods, tilts my head. 'Oh, there'll be that, alright. Plenty more green put your way. And I suppose you'll be banking it as well?'

A smile. Another nod. It takes another wee sip on the half-pint, seems to be getting used to it now. 'Yes.'

I leans back in my seat and folds my arms behind my head. My mind's off in the clouds, chasing rainbows, and then there's an almighty blast on a trumpet just south of my ear.

'Hey, what's with the fucking racket?' I goes.

The old bastard looks at me like I've just picked his pocket.

'Right, come on, drink up. We've got things to talk about.'

It looks a bit startled, pats about on the seat for its bag and scarf and that. 'We are leaving?'

'Aye, aye. Come on,' I goes. 'Let's have a sketch at this flat of yours.'

*****

I can't take much more of this.

It's like there's a boulder on my chest, like I'm trapped. But I know it's not a boulder. It's Jonesy.

'Get the fuck off me!' I roars out.

He doesn't move; he's laughing. 'Aye, you don't like that, do you?'

He's not talking to me, he's playing to the crowd.

'They like giving it out but can't take it,' one of them roars.

Who's they?

'They don't like it up them.'

'Who's they?' I say the words this time.

There's a slap. I feel my teeth clatter. It's not a hand that slaps me. I look up and Jonesy has the cricket stump in his hand. 'You know where this is going, don't you?'

'Fuck off,' I yell at him.

I get another slap. The other side of the face this time. My jaw cracks and the muscles of my neck scream out in agony.

'Where's the smart mouth now, you wee stoat?' goes Jonesy.

I can hear a scatter of voices, all around me, from the crowd. I look over and I know the faces. Every one. There's Uncle Barry, my mother's half-brother. There's Blue Peter who sells the under-the-counter porno. There's Eck, the slowman, who doesn't know why he's there. There's Christine, my first ride. There's Len the scaffie, holding one of those wee teddy bears that's usually pinned to the front of the bin-wagon. There's Mr Mair, my old PE teacher, shaking his head and just about turning away, but something's keeping him there. And there's Peggy, the ginger bitch from the chippy that was taking a length off my Old Boy until he got put away. It's got the hard, pinched face of all Glasgow bitches that have a wrong to right. Peggy sees me staring and unfolds the arms over its stomach, leans out. 'Just like your father!' It spits on me. I try to move away but I feel the vile gob spray into my eyes. 'Just like your fucking father!' it roars. 'A wee fucking stoat.'

I look away but all I see is Jonesy. He's got my shoulders pinned down now. Not by him. The others have joined in. 'Get his breeks off,' goes Jonesy.

The others pile on. The whole crowd start pulling at me, ripping my clothes. 'Get the fuck off!' I goes. 'Leave me.'

'Come on, right down around the ankles,' goes Jonesy.

I feel my heart thumping, so fast I think it's going to jump out my chest. I feel hot then cold all over. I want to call out, to scream, but all my words have left me. I've forgotten how to speak, how to make a noise even. As I look up, Jonesy's smiling, a great wide grin splitting his face in two. He has the cricket stump in one hand and he's slapping it in the other.

I hear a loud voice break through the racket: 'No.'

Everyone stops still. My head is clamped to the ground and as I try to get a view of where the voice has come from, all I can see is Jonesy's face. 'What the fuck?' he goes.

The figure steps into view — it's a broad-backed man — and as he knocks the cricket stump out of Jonesy's hand; he speaks up again, 'You want this.' I recognise the voice now. I can hardly believe what I'm hearing as the broad-backed man hands Jonesy a red-hot poker, the tip glowing amber and smoking like it's just been pulled from a flame.

'You beauty!' goes Jonesy.

As he takes the poker in his hand, he raises it to the sky and the crowd roar out.

'Do it!'

'Now!'

'Up the arse!'

I'm frozen, rooted in fear as the broad-backed man turns round and I see my father's face. The thin slits of his eyes burning right into me.

'Stauner!'

I see him speak to me, but the voice isn't his.

'Stauner!'

It's a lassie's voice.

'Stauner!'

A foreign voice.

'Wake up. You're screaming. Wake up.'

I open my eyes and see Monique sitting on the bed.

I'm soaked in sweat, but it doesn't seem to mind.

I push its arms away, and dive to the side because I can't stand eyes on me.

'Fuck off,' I goes. 'Just fucking-well leave me alone.'

*****

I can tell it's taken the hook, well and truly like, when it starts bubbling away. I mean lassies don't need any encouragement on that front, sight of a poorly kitten or a bit of chipped nail varnish and the sprinklers go on. But this one's putting the powerhose to shame as it follows me down the street in the baffies. It grabs at my arm, but I jerk it away. It grabs again and I jerk harder – it's not got the picture, bit slow on the uptake – the next step is the fist drawn back. Threat of a split lip always does the trick.

'No, please don't hit me!' It cowers back and crouches down, the big pink Peppa Pig baffies get scrunched up and it looks like the daft sow's snorting away on the pavement with them. I have to do a double take, when the hands go up around the head, defensive like.

'Get up off that street!'

'I'm sorry ... I'm sorry ...'

The tears are still coming, still rolling down the cheeks, when I jerk it to its feet. 'What d'you think you're playing at, eh?' It stares down. 'Trying to get me lifted?' I points up to the CCTV camera over the road. 'Mr Bacon's always watching. Not enough for you I nearly got put away last night?'

'I'm sorry!' it goes again, louder this time, pure dead anxious, so it is. Thinks the bold Stauner's truly walking out on it. I feels a wee belt of pride knowing I've got it so wound up.

'And you can quit that shite, right now.' I pinches my lips and makes a mocking face and a girly voice, '*I'm sorry ... I'm sorry ...* you sound like a broken record. so you do, and not a good one, bloody Kylie Minogue or something.'

It straightens up and wipes the eyes, starts to shiver because it's still morning and Glasgow after all. I watch it, pure broken before me, and I'm thinking this one's been through the mill. Had it hard. Likely that ex-boyfriend of hers has been a bastard-and-a-half; I know right away I can use this to my advantage. The daft bitch will be eating out my hand from here on, totally scared of a repeat performance. See, it'll remember the pain of losing the last bloke, remember the heartache, and not want to repeat it. I see now this ex has done me a favour and in all fairness I should shake his hand. The facts of life, likes.

'Please, Stauner,' its voice drops now. 'Please, just don't ...' It reaches out and places a delicate little tap on my elbow.

'Get off!' I jerks my arm away, ups the volume as I set it straight. 'You think I'm putting up with your carry on?'

It shakes its head. The arms get folded, not in the normal way – one over the other – but actually around its waist, like it's trying to cuddle itself. 'I– I–' It looks for the right words, but it knows – and I know

– that it was going to say sorry again. I turns for the road. 'No, please wait ... I'll do anything you say.'

Bingo!

And that's what Stauner's been waiting to hear. Fair play to myself, it has to be said, got this one puggled in the head already.

'What you on about ... *anything*?'

It's shivering with the cold again. 'Anything. Just, please, don't leave.'

'Don't leave?'

'Please ...'

I leans over it, points the finger at its nose. 'See me, no lassie tells me what to do. I'm a free agent. I come and go as I please.'

'Of course.'

'So, don't be telling me what to say or do.'

'No. I would never.'

I steps back, lowers the finger. For some reason I'm pure gasping for a fag. 'Got any money?'

It shakes its head. 'Only back at my apartment.'

'No good to me here, is it?' I rolls my eyes. 'I'm wanting a fag, now. See what you've done to me? Got me gantin for nicotine.'

It takes a step back, tries to encourage me to turn back the way we came. 'I will go and get you cigarettes, please, come back home with me. I'll get some money.'

I like the sound of this. See, thing is, when you've got them dipping into their purse that's when the hook's really in. Really, really in. Well and truly in, so it is. The facts of life, likes.

*****

For a good couple of weeks the future's so bright I've gotta wear shades. I've got the French bint running about after me day and night. There's food in the fridge and Sky Sports on the telly. The Stauner's feet are well and truly under the table. I even manage to forget about the two great blocks of doobie I left behind in my old bedsit.

The routine I've settled into is much the same as when I was creaming it in at the Boneyard. I gets out the pit at midday – Monique's usually still out for the count after working the night for Geddes – and checks in with my turf accountant. Folk say the ponies is a mug's game, but that's just mugs themselves talking. There has to be winners and losers in every game. And it's not like I'm betting my own money. The Old Boy would have been proud to see the job I'd done on this bint. Proud as punch, so he would.

The ScotBet's crowded with punters putting a line on the one o'clock at Ayr. I've got an accumulator on, sitting pretty with a win already scratched up, when I start to feel a wee bit funny. It's like I'm being watched, like there's eyes burning into me. I turns round but can't see anyone looking my way. I'm thinking: That's a bit strange. I give myself a wee shake and put it down to someone crossing my grave – then out of the blue there's a hand on my back.

'Alright, mate.'

I have to take a step back when I clock who's just appeared. My breath shortens and I hardly recognise my voice when I speak, 'Jonesy ...' For a moment I'm off guard, and that's not like me, not one wee bit. I reach for something else to say, a conversation starter, but my mind isn't working. My breathing shortens further, seems to stop.

'Christ, don't look so shocked, Stauner, it's my home town as well.'

My eyes start to blink quickly. 'But, I thought you left ...'

Yes, Jonesy left.

He left some time ago.

When I think of why he left I feel a tightening in the pit of my stomach and then a cold bead of sweat runs the length of my spine.

He smiles. 'I did that. And I've been all over the world since,' he taps the side of his nose and winks, '... seen a thing or two, let me tell you, mate.'

His words flash past me like bullets, seem too fast

for me to take in. My mind is awash with thoughts that I've tried to forget for years. Sounds and images return that I had buried long ago. I try to flush them out, to concentrate on what I need to know about the here and now.

I want to know why he's in Glasgow.

I want to know if he's planning on sticking around.

I want to ask him about a lot of things, but I can't bring myself to because it's just too difficult to look him in the eye. And he knows it.

'But nothing compares to the Dear Green Place, isn't that right ... Stauner?' He says my name like I've never heard it said before, like it means something to him that it doesn't mean to anyone else.

I don't know what to reply. I feel like running. The nightmares flash to the front of my mind. The sight of Jonesy with the cricket stump, with the red-hot poker, get reeled out. I gulp some air and nod to him. He steps aside as I shuffle away, head for the door.

'Be seeing you around, old mate,' calls Jonesy. 'Maybe grab you for a pint one night.'

His words are ringing in my ears as I leave the bookies and start to hurry up the street. My heart's pounding. I can feel a stabbing pain in the back of my calves as I go; it's like my legs are about to fold under me.

The fuck's wrong with me? I'm thinking as I start to push my way through the crowded pavement. There's a gale blowing and my hair's all over the place, but I leave it be. I want to be away from people. I want to be out of sight. I don't want to be around another living soul, just on my own, in hiding. I know it's an instinct: fight or flight, they call it.

'Jesus Christ!' I mutter as I try to get the key in the door to the flat. My hands are shaking as I spring the lock and go inside. I press my back against the door as it closes and slide down to the bottom. The stair is cold and grey; no lights are working. I feel a shiver pass through me and it makes my shoulders shoogle.

'Jesus fucking Christ,' I goes. 'Jonesy! Fucking Jonesy!'

I need to move, I need to be somewhere where I know there's no chance of him finding me. I try to raise myself but my legs are like jelly. My knees buckle as I get on my feet and then I sway — left to right — as I head for the stairs. I think for a moment I'm going to hurl. I can feel it rising in me. Breakfast repeating: the slice-sausage rolls from Sweaty Betty's.

'Urgh ...'

The sound of my chucking up in the stair brings Monique out. It rushes to my side. 'Darling, what is it?'

I pushes it away. 'Nothing!'

'But you've been sick.'

'It's nothing,' I goes. 'Get that fucking mess cleaned up.'

I edge past it, lean into the banister as I make my way up the stairs. Each leg raised from step to step feels like it's made of cement. I want to stop and sit, but more than anything I want to hide. I want to hide from Jonesy.

*****

For three days I hole up in the flat. I watch wall-to-wall telly. Brain-dead stuff. I want to kill Phillip Schofield. There is not a single reason that I can think of that will shift me. Even when I run out of Dax hair wax and I have to use crappy gel on the sides, I wait in for Monique to bring more back from the shops. It's a sad state of affairs for the Stauner, but the option is ... what?

'This cannot go on,' goes Monique.

'Eh, what do you mean?' I'm thinking it's going on about me turning into a houseplant, but then it surprises me.

'We need to talk.'

'We are talking.'

It rises from the chair and comes to my side on the sofa. 'I mean, darling, we need to talk about what happened to make you sick the other day ... and why you have not been outside since.'

I gives it a look, one that lets it know that the mark

has been overstepped. It retreats a wee bit, crosses fingers and drops gaze. 'I'm sorry. I only want to help.'

I huffs: 'And how're you going to do that?'

'Anything ... anything.'

It starts to yak away about not being happy if I'm not happy and if there was one thing it could do to change things for me all I need to do is say. It goes on and on about this and that and the next thing, and then it comes up with something that catches my attention.

'What did you say there?'

'I said, if I had the money I would take you away from here, somewhere where you would be happy.'

I turns the Stauner charm up, smile at it and goes, 'Oh, aye ... tell me more.'

'I would take you far, far away ...'

'Where?'

It starts to brighten because it sees it's got my attention. 'Paris! ... I'd take you to my favourite city and make you happy there.'

I grips the hand I'm holding. 'Sounds nice.'

'And I would show you around, let you meet all my friends and we would live happily ever after.'

I goes for broke, picks up its hand and puts a wee kiss on the back. 'But, doll, all that costs money.'

The smile drops from its face. The black eyes look gloomy and dark. 'I know.' Monique turns to stare out the window, looks like it's searching for ideas. 'I could save my money, from the Boneyard.'

I shakes my head. 'On your wages, that'd take forever and a day.'

I watch the disappointment spread across its face. There's two thin white lines around the edges of its mouth where its smile was sitting a moment ago. 'Maybe I could ask Mr Geddes for a rise, and I could save hard and then we could go to ...'

I drops its hand. 'Listen to yourself ... the only rise

you're getting out of Davie Geddes is in his decrepit old prick!'

Monique's head drops. It knows I'm right, knows I speak sense. As I mention his name I feel my pulse quicken. I'm still sore about the fact that the bastard put me in this fucking boat. If I was still dealing in the Boneyard I'd have a nice wee pile of notes tucked away in the sky rocket and hanging about Glasgow to bump into Jonesy wouldn't be an issue. I'd be Harry the Toff. Off to Paris or anywhere I fucking-well pleased.

I jumps off the sofa. 'Right, here's what we're going to do. I want you to get your bag packed!'

'What?' It looks scoobied, pure didn't see that one coming.

'You heard, doll, I want your bags packed and I want the tickets bought for Paris.'

Its eyes widen as I speak. It's off the sofa and following me about the flat with the hands waving and the hair flouncing about with the headshakes. 'But I don't understand ... Paris. I know we can't afford to go.'

'Yes we can.' I stops it flat, grips the thin arms in my hands and puts a bead on it. 'Listen to me, that cunt Geddes owes me. He fucked me over and now it's our chance to fuck him back.'

It shakes its head. 'But how?'

I have to shake my own head cos I can't believe the penny hasn't dropped. 'Jesus fucking Christ, have you not got the picture yet? What have you been doing for Geddes for the last few weeks? You've been serving his punters, ringing up his tills and ... banking his cash!'

'Yes, it is all true.'

I can't stop a big smile spreading over my coupon as I deliver the plan that's been brewing inside me since I first clocked it with the cash bag in Starbucks. 'Right, well, no fucking more, doll. I want you to stop banking the cash and start building a stash!'

It takes the plan better than I thought. I expected some resistance, to do some persuading, but the Stauner's got this one under the fucking thumb. 'Yes,

yes ... and then we could go to Paris.'

'We could go this fucking week! Just a matter of days ...'

It actually jumps at the notion. 'We could be in Paris by the weekend.' It runs to me and throws arms round me, plants a big smacker on my lips.

'Whoa, whoa ... cool the beans. We've got some planning to do. Sort yourself out and get me a pen and paper. Stauner's going to show you how to take Geddes to the fucking cleaners.'

*****

It was like it had no clue, no fucking clue at all.

I watches Monique get into Geddes's big BMW and turn the key in the ignition. The car splutters and dies.

'Jesus Christ.'

On the second attempt the Beemer bites, then it bunny-hops the motor out the park and onto the road. It dies again.

'Fucking hellfire.' I shakes my head as I stands in the side street over the road. It's like the bint's trying to get caught, like it's wearing a sign round the neck that reads:

YO, GEDDES, I'M THINKING OF POCKETING THIS LOT

By the third go, it gets the motor chugging along; drives it to the traffic lights at the end of the road and chucks a U-turn. It's a shonky enough turn, it has to be said, but we're talking about a 7-Series BMW and a lassie at the wheel, so fair fucks.

Monique must have been tipping 20mph when the brakes get slammed on — some cunt in a Clio at the rear slams his hand on the horn — I shake my head again and watch the Beemer pull up outside The Spar. It's still got a face that's tripping it, white as a sheet, and twitching like fucking Bambi in the cross-hairs when I lobs out of my hidey-hole and pulls open the passenger door.

'That was some fucking performance, doll,' I goes.

I jumps in and it floors the pedal and pulls off. 'I have the nerves, you know.'

'Aye, so I see.' I leans back in the leather chair; good to see Geddes has splashed for the full-leather inside. Wasted on him, like; now, if it was me, I'd be at the riding every other night with a motor like this, but Geddes is pure past it. Likely needs the Viagra or a pump attached to a bell-jar to get it up. 'Some motor this, eh?'

It's gripping the wheel like its life depends on it, like it's hanging off the edge of a cliff or that. 'Pardon?'

'Pardon ...' I goes. Have to correct it, the way it speaks is pure daftie stuff sometimes, like it can't grasp the lingo. 'It's pardon! ... Not *pwar-dohn*!'

'Yes. I know. Sorry.'

I runs a hand over the dash, nice bit of wood in there, all varnished up and that. 'Nice wood, eh?' I goes, like it'll know what I'm on about.

'Yes, I like the walnut.'

'Walnut ... what you on about? It's the wood there I'm talking about.' I slaps the dash and I'm pure tempted to give it a wee belt as well, just because I'm getting rattled with it now.

It looks at me with those slanty eyes, from the side like, and I tell it to keep the eyes on the road. 'Where are we going?'

I looks out the back window, makes sure there's no one following us — like one of Geddes's daft pug-lads in the trackies — but there's no one. I knew he wouldn't have the marbles to suspect it. See, that's the difference with me: I suspect everyone, cos you never know who's going to screw you over. Trust no one is the only way. The facts of life, likes.

'Just you keep driving, do as we planned ...'

'So, to the bank, yes.'

'Aye. The bank, same one you always head for ... don't be changing the route either, same way you always go or you'll be attracting suspicion to us and that's the last thing we want. Got it?'

It starts to nod. 'Yes. I have got it.'

'Good. That's what I want to hear. You just leave all the thinking to me.'

The traffic is busy, loads of silly wee wifey-types in big 4x4 motors. They're all stuffed full of wee brats, spoiled wee bairns that might as well be sucking on silver spoons. I look them up and down, clock their motors and shake my head just to noise them up. See those cows, all about the bawbees, all about the showing off the big house and the big motor. None of them have a set of wheels like this, though. I'll give Geddes that much: he knows how to piss the posh sows off. I get a right buzz out of sitting in the car when the traffic's come to a standstill and all the snobby bitches start taking a sketch at the big Beemer. I feel like hanging out the window and screaming at them, 'Not in your fucking dreams, doll!'

We reach the bank and there's a space outside, well, nearly outside – more like at the bakers next door.

'Right. You know the routine, aye?' I goes.

It nods, rapid-style. 'Yes, same as I do every day, but this time only pay in a little amount.'

'A hundred. Get me? Just one hundred.'

'Okay. Yes. I understand.'

I leans forward, grabs it by the arm. 'And get the pay-in slip. You'll need that to give to Geddes when you go back.'

'I will remember, yes.'

It's starting to panic, and I know it's about to fuck things up if it doesn't get a grip. It grabs the door handle and heads out. I lean over and pull it back inside the motor. 'Hey, what the fuck are you doing?'

It slaps its brow, smiles at me. 'How silly ...'

'That's one way of putting it,' I goes. 'Hand it over.'

I takes the cash bag off it and removes the bundle of cash. Mostly fives and tens, but a few twenties as well. It's a fair wad. 'Eleven gees, eh?'

'Yes.'

I hands it back a hundred in tens and nods it on its way. I'm seriously contemplating knocking ten bells out it for this performance, but I just takes note that it'll need a proper talking to later if it's not to blow our cover.

As Monique heads to the bank I tucks the green in my Ben Sherman and tries to look relaxed. I spot a fat bastard stuffing his face with a pasty from Greggs, brown sauce dripping off it and onto his chin as he heads for his white van. When he waddles off I see the plaster covering his dungarees and I think what is wrong with the man? I'm not bothered about the plaster, manky as that is – a man has to make a living – but it's the uniform of the lesbian that upsets me. Dungarees is the slippery slope. Next is the Doc Martens and the Number 1 to the napper. It's horrific, the thought of a grown man kitted up like a dyke, but it only reminds me why I have such a good record with the lassies. I mean, when the competition looks like fucking Sandi Toksvig you can expect to score every time.

Monique comes darting out the bank like it's just held the place up and jumps into the Beemer. It leans back gasping for air and that's when I noticed how flushed its cheeks are, pure red, working like bellows.

'What the fuck's wrong?' I goes.

It doesn't answer, just starts to fumble with the keys.

'Eh, what happened?' I goes.

The ignition bites and suddenly the Beemer's lunging forward and we're on the road with a hail of horns going at the back of us. I looks back – half expecting to see a security guard or a copper taking aim at us – but there's no sign of any commotion on the street. It's still gulping the air down and trembling about the mouth and I starts to realise that maybe I've not picked the best partner for this caper. Maybe the thought of turning over Geddes is going to be all a wee bit too much for this daft lassie.

*****

There's folk that can handle the pressure, and there's those that just can't. The facts of life, likes. When I was at the school there was all these square-peg cunts that would panic and fret over the exams and that, had themselves worked up to a state of high doh so they did, and then there was the bold Stauner. Not for the likes of me, the old panic. No, sir. Whilst every other daftie was away home to get at the studying and greeting themselves to sleep every night over their papers and books, I was out and about.

'Come on!' I goes. Got a horse in the 3.30 at Kelso. 'That's the way ... all the way!' The filly has its nose out in front and I'm thinking the black bastard to the rear is edging closer and we might see a photo-finish.

'Go yourself!' goes wee Ally Hamilton.

'Come on!'

Wee Ally grabs onto my shoulder and starts to heave himself up. I'm not overly chuffed about this because I don't want anyone to be thinking I'm an arse-bandit. 'Hey, come on t'fuck!' I tells him.

Wee Ally clocks the look on me and removes his mitt. 'Sorry, and all that.'

'Better,' I goes.

There's a rush of adrenalin around the bookies

and then there's an uproar as my pony comes in.

'Y'fucking dancer!' I goes and wee Ally's punching the air beside me.

We grab our winnings and then it's back to the Racing Post and picking out the next challenger.

'That's easy money that,' goes wee Ally.

'Easy as taking sweeties off a bairn,' I tells him.

'Oh, aye ... like taking the bairn's money at Tatty Tait's back in the day. Remember that?'

He's talking about the corner shop we used to hang about in down the scheme when we were boys. There was always a bit of green to be had from going in for the carry-outs for the underagers.

'The bairns and their bevy,' I goes.

'Aye, the wee schoolies more like,' goes Ally. 'Always fun to be had with the wee schoolies!' He starts laughing it up, then he's elbowing me and winking. 'They were the days, Stauner, eh?'

'Oh, aye ...' I goes. 'Sound days, Ally.' Some said those wee tarts were too young to be out drinking and that, but who're they to judge? Just cos it's the rule of the land doesn't mean those wee prick-teasers didn't know what they were playing at.

'Had some good rides on the crates at the back of the shop,' goes wee Ally. He's at it, playing up, just trying to big note himself. I know for sure and certain this wee fannybaws can count his rides on one hand – and the ride of his life likely was his hand.

'Is that right, Ally?'

He nods at me, has a wee cheesy smirk on his coupon that says he's trying to creep in with me. 'Aye, some of them were better than others, mind you.'

I'm thinking of telling him that a bad ride's still better than a good wank, but I don't think he'd know the difference. 'Well, I've never had to bag it yet, Ally ... not catch me going for the munters.'

He looks at me like I've just given him a peach of a backhander, like I've knocked his glasses off and his expression into next week. He looks none too chuffed and starts to spark up a bit. 'Aye well, if you keep to the schoolies then it's an unfair advantage.'

I've heard this patter before. I'm having none of it. I points the finger and digs it into his chest. 'If there's grass on the pitch – let's play ... that's what I say.'

That shuts him up. Pure wipes the crabbit face off him as well. I'm thinking he knows better than to mess with the likes of me, but from somewhere he gets a second wind. 'Aye well, I'm not saying you're wrong or that, but all I will say is this: I met a boy in here the other day who would disagree with you.' Wee Ally keeps his head low, starts poring over the form pages. I waits for another word from him, something that will give some meaning to what he's just said, but nothing comes.

Against my better judgement, I plays into Ally's hands. 'And, eh, who would that be ... that would disagree with me?'

Wee Ally's face doesn't move as he starts to scratch a blunt pencil on the back of a dud receipt. I'm thinking he's not going to reply, just ding me, but then the pale lips start to move. 'It was a face I hadn't seen in a long while.' He looks up, makes sure he's got me in full view then he goes: 'A face you know well enough.'

I know he's at it. I know wee Ally thinks he's pulling some kind of rank on me because he's got a bit of information that he wants to flaunt. I know the way to deal with this kind of cuntery is to let it lie, to let the wee arsehole keep his silly wee secret to himself and just watch as it fizzles out of him and then pay it no heed. But I can't. I want to stick to the rules, to watch wee Ally hang himself, but the other option's playing in the back of my mind because I have to know if my suspicions will be confirmed.

My heart rate ramps as I start to speak. 'Go on then ... *Who*?'

Wee Ally can't believe his luck, can't believe he has me by the ball-hairs. 'Well, as I say, it's a face you know well enough ...' He pauses, makes sure he has me in his gaze and milks my attention for all it's worth. 'Because we were all at the school together.'

I'm tempted to lamp him one.

The bookies suddenly becomes very warm.

I feel the need for cold air. I want to open a window.

It must be on my face that I'm about to bolt because then wee Ally sparks up again. 'It was Jonesy!'

I knew it. I just knew it. But somehow I needed to hear it confirmed. For a moment I feel a flash of heat inside my head. I'd almost forgotten meeting Jonesy a few days ago — well, had tried to forget. When I hear his name I feel the same nausea that engulfs me during the nightmares, but I try to fight it. I know I can't be seen to give an inch to Jonesy in front of wee Ally because that would get around the town like wildfire.

I clamps down my emotions and tries to play it straight. 'Oh, aye, and why would Jonesy be disagreeing with me, then?'

Wee Ally smirks. I can see the tobacco-stained, jagged little points of his broken teeth and then he goes, 'Well, seeing as how you were that friendly way with his wee sister back then, maybe he might be taking a different view is all I'm saying ...' He pauses, puts the face on he'd shown me earlier. 'Especially now, like, after what happened.'

I watch wee Ally tip his head back. He's gone beyond milking information from me and now he's getting ready to floor me. He has something bigger than the news that Jonesy's back in town to get at me with and now I see that. The wee bastard has been storing it up. He's been purposely playing up to me. All the small chat, the laughing and joking. He's been trying to reel me in. He's been slowly turning the conversation round to the subject now in question. He's had a plan, that started long before he visited the bookies, to put this on me. He's a bastard, a malicious wee chattering bastard who wants nothing more than to see the look on my face when he utters his bit of fucking gossip so that he can take it away and tell some other wee chattering gossip bastard.

I want to turn around and walk out.

I want to tighten my jaw and play dumb. To look uninterested.

I want to blow out wee Ally and leave the bookies with my dignity intact.

But I can't.

I play into his hands. 'After what happened?' I goes.

'Oh, you never heard ... about Jonesy's wee sister?'

'Heard what?'

'I thought you'd have heard ... you of all folk, since you were so *close*, like.'

'Heard what, Ally?'

He squares his shoulders, coughs into his fist to clear his throat, and goes: 'She killed herself.'

*****

I gets back to the flat and parks it on the sofa. My mind is full of Jonesy and his wee sister, and I'm churning up inside. But of course this fucking daft bint is at me already, running around and trying to loosen off my boots as soon as I'm in the door.

'Just fucking leave it, eh?' I goes.

'What is wrong, darling?'

What's wrong? Like it could contemplate. Like it has any idea what I'm thinking after the news that wee cunt Ally just delivered in the ScotBet. 'Never you fucking mind, what's wrong,' I goes. 'And what have I told you about letting me get in the door and seated without bringing me a bevy?'

It jumps up, scrunches the coupon and goes, 'Oh, I'm sorry. I forgot.'

'Aye well, sorry isn't putting a tin in my hand, is it?' I puts the hand out, makes the shape of a grip going round a tin. It gets the picture, slowly right enough, but it's only a lassie and I've got to remind myself of that over and over.

As it spins off to the kitchen I start to get the boots off. I mean, it's already loosened the laces so I might as well. My head is thumping to add to my woes and my mind is just awash with images of wee Janie Jones in its younger days. It was such a braw wee lassie. A right wee goer as well, so it was. As I bend over I feel a tightness in my chest that I've never felt before and suddenly I have to lean back on the sofa. I'm thinking, That's a bit strange. But then, my whole life's been in turmoil these last few weeks and there's the stress to consider. Aye, that'll be it, I tells myself. Nothing but stress, nothing a few chugs on a good bevy won't sort.

I wriggles my feet out the boots and drags the wee footstool thing over and I'm starting to calm down a bit, the chest pains subsiding, when in walks Monique and I can feel the eyes just about bursting out my head. I really don't believe what I'm seeing – I jump to my feet and put both hands in the air in sheer disbelief.

'What in the fucking wide world of sports is that?'

It looks at me, then shakes its head. It says something in French and that just gets my goat even more.

'I've fuckingwell told you about using that frog lingo in this house!'

It looks at me and I'm thinking it's contemplating saying, 'But hang on, this is my house.' But then I remember it would be far wide of the mark for it to start at that patter; I mean, this is a lassie that knows which side its bread's buttered on.

'I'm sorry, I forgot ...' it goes.

'Forgot what ... about the frog lingo, or about the bevy?'

Now it's scoobied and just starts to nod and goes, 'Yes. Yes.'

I walks over to it and swipes the tin right out its hand. The bint's nearly rocked on its heels as I reach forward and start on it. 'The fuck is this?' I goes, pointing at the tin of vileness. 'Fucking Guinness. Are you taking the fucking piss, eh? Is that it?'

'I'm sorry, I don't understand,' it goes, and the bottom lip is sticking out just like a bairn's before it starts to bubble.

I shakes the tin, a few splashes of its vileness lands on the carpet, but I am beyond caring. 'Fucking Guinness! And me a season-ticket holder at Rangers for these last ten years!' I can feel my face heating. There's spit coming from my mouth and landing in its face. 'Guinness? For a true blue Billy Boy like me ... you're taking the piss, aren't you?'

It looks to the left, then to the right. I watch it trying to find somewhere to land the eyeballs because it knows there's nowhere for it to hide in the whole room. It speaks up, 'I still don't understand.'

I feel like I'm talking to a brick wall. 'Jesus Christ ... I'm surprised you never brought it through with a wee bowl of Hula Hoops!'

It starts to gnaw on the bottom lip now. It's beyond scoobied and I'm beyond trying to educate it. I mean, if a good Rangers man can't have a tin under his own roof after a hard day down the bookies then the world has changed in ways that I cannot fathom.

'I give up,' I goes.

It just stands there, looking glaiket as I head out the door and slam it behind me.

I gets out into the hall and the dark unsettles me for some reason; I puts on the light but the bulb shatters – it makes me jump. I shudder a little and quickly pad it through to the bedroom. I'm relieved to see that the light is still working here and that it's not a fuse that's blown, because one fuse blown in this place tonight is well and truly enough.

I park it on the edge of the bed and I can still feel my pulse racing in my arms. The pain in my chest is still there, beginning to peak a bit now as I check the rest of the room for evidence that Monique might be a Tim on the fly. There's a green bottle on the dresser that looks like deodorant and there's a pair of green knickers I haven't seen before hanging on the radiator and both items start to annoy me so much by the very sight of them that I have to lift them and fling them under the bed.

'Fucking bastards.' I can't bring myself to say the name of the team. It's been years since I've stooped that low and I won't allow the actions of a stupid wee French lassie to disrupt my discipline. I am a man of principle after all. The facts of life, likes.

I flops back on the bed and I'm starting to feel my surging blood settle when I hear the door creak and then I clock the shamed face slinking through the door and parking it on the edge of the bed.

'Stauner, I am so sorry ... I will try harder to remember all that you tell me in future.'

'Aye, you better start, cos you're running out of chances, doll.' It knows it's done wrong and all that so there's no point forcing home the issue. It's like rubbing a dog's nose in it, and that caper never does any good. Might make you feel a bit better, but it doesn't help the dog's training and that's the bigger picture that you have to consider. Dogs and lassies need to be encouraged to the right kind of behaviour and if you wield the big stick too often it's just no use. I mean, nobody likes to see a dog that's been beaten too much or a lassie that's afraid of its own shadow. There's a line to be drawn, and right enough, sometimes it's a fine line, but it's a line that has to be observed.

'I am sorry,' it goes. 'I promise it won't happen again.'

I feel myself pressing the inside of my cheek with the tip of my tongue; I've been doing this a lot lately and I'm wondering if it's a nervous thing when I snap myself out of it. 'Right, right ... just learn your lesson and stop creeping about me.'

It leans over and starts to cuddle up to me on the bed. I'm not interested in getting the bobby right now, so I edges it away and it takes the hint.

'Stauner, have you counted up today's cash?'

'Of course I have.' One of us has got to keep ahead of the game.

'How much do we have?'

'It's all looking good and that's all you need to know.'

It falls silent, then: 'It must be over £50,000.'

I turns over and looks at it. 'Aye, it must be. It's Saturday tomorrow and we've got nearly a whole week's takings sitting under the bed.'

Monique starts to smile. 'I have packed. Have you?'

'What's to pack?'

'Your things ... don't you want to take them to Paris?'

I shakes my head. 'Nah, I'm going to travel light. I'll get new gear in Paris. With the money likes, get some new Ben Sherman gear, best of stuff like.'

It smiles at me and I can tell it's fair taken by the idea of us moving to Paris. It's just like any other lassie, thinks every step I take in life is on the same road as it's got in its head of Mr and Mrs Perfect with the white picket fence and all that. I mean, stroll on. I'll take the shift over the water to Paris and all that, but I'll be fucked if any bint is getting its hooks into the bold Stauner. Free agent and all that. Facts of life, likes.

'Are you excited?' it goes.

'Naw, I'm not.'

'Not one little bit? Not even at the thought of all the money? We only have the weekend to go and then we will flee.'

The thought makes me smile. Just one more night's worth of takings and then we're off. Davie

Geddes won't know what's hit him. I can see the bastard's face when it suddenly dawns on him that Monique isn't coming back. That it's taken him to the cleaners.

'Aye, well,' I goes. 'When you put it like that, I suppose you could say I'm a wee bit excited.'

It leaps on the bed and straddles me, starts the hard-core French kissing, and I'm thinking, why the fuck not, eh? Why the fuck not? But as it flicks out the bedside light I get the strangest sensation that it's not Monique I'm kissing but wee Janie Jones.

'Ahh,' I yells out. 'Get the fuck off me!'

'What is it?' it goes.

I'm shaking and trembling as I reach for the light switch. 'Nothing ... just leave me.'

'But you are as white as the sheet.'

'I said just fucking leave it, eh?' I gets out of the bed and heads into the hallway, closing the door behind me. I feel suddenly very alone as I stand there wondering what the fuck is going on inside my head.

*****

Sleep is out the question for another night — the nightmares just ruling it right out — so I sends Monique for some more tins. I tells it to get the good stuff this time, McEwan's, and to take a trip to the Chinkies: the only place open at this time of the night, otherwise I'd be avoiding it like a dose of Aids.

Pure chucking it down outside, but it's not my fault it doesn't own an umbrella; only fucking lassie I've ever known doesn't have at least five umbrellas about the house. I told it to get me chips and curry sauce and a bag of banana fritters. Only two things safe to get off Chinkies; not risking the chicken, which every cunt knows is really cat or rat or that. Well known for it, they are, hear all kinds of stories about folk finding deep-fried dog collars in these places. And big Sammy from the Buck's Head says he's seen the Chinkie cunts trapping pigeons on George Square in the middle of the night; well, they're not doing that for a laugh.

My Old Boy was the same, couldn't stick any foreign muck. Always said he was a meat and potatoes man and I'm the same. I just wonder what he'd have made of me pushing off to France with Monique. Some dodgy muck on offer there, frog's legs and all that. Mind you, he'd have been all over the French lassies like a rash. He'd be like a rat up a fucking drainpipe, the dirty old bastard. I has a wee smile to myself thinking about some of the gash he tried to pull in his day – some of it mine, as well – and I just know I'm a chip off the old block in many ways.

I'm still thinking about the Old Boy when it strolls in with the hair all dripping wet and the clothes sticking to it like it's been swimming in the Clyde.

'Hello, darling,' it goes. 'I have the correct beer this time.'

'Aye well, it better be.' I holds my hand out for the stripy blue and white carrier bag – least that's a good start – and takes a deck inside. Six tins all lined up. I puts my hand in and grabs one.

'Not the coldest,' I goes.

'Oh, there was no fridge there ... I had to walk to the 24-hour garage because everywhere else was closed.'

I shakes my head and takes a tin, cracks the ring-pull. 'Nothing worse than warm lager, y'know.'

It starts wiping the rain off its forehead and then it goes, 'I'll put some in the freezer, soon as I get out of these wet clothes.'

'Whoa ... wait a minute. Get your priorities straight: you can get changed any time. Get those tins in the freezer first. Christ on a bike, do I have to do everything around here?'

It shuffles off to the kitchen with the eyes downward, dripping water all over the floor. 'I am sorry. The beer will be nice and cold soon, yes.'

I hates the way it puts that 'yes' on the end there, no fucking need for it. But I lets it go by because it doesn't pay to be at it all the day long. 'Aye, so they will.'

It comes back from the kitchen with the Daddies sauce in its hand and I'm thinking I've done alright with the training here. I smothers the chips in sauce and gets fired in. I'm disappointed there's no footy on the telly and have to settle for some snooker. Some fat wee cunt and an Aussie with ridiculous spiky hair are playing. He looks like that Marti Pellow from back in the day when everyone in Glasgow was just reeking ashamed of that band of his for that Number 1 they had. Mind you, he'd grown the pony tail by then and it has to be said that was a touch of class. But this snooker gadgie is well shy of that level. I just despair at the state of some blokes; ones on the telly as well, with all that opportunity to get the lassies and they throw it away with a head like a lavvy brush. I runs my fingers through the famous Stauner locks and know I'm a class act myself; pure fucking class. The facts of life, likes.

It comes back through looking all pleased with itself after remembering the sauce bottle, but this time it's got a plate for the Chinkie. I brushes it aside. 'A plate for a take away, you off your scone, hen?'

It looks at me all scoobied and stands there holding the big white plate like a bairn pretending to drive a lorry or something. 'But, I thought ...'

I raises the hand, shuts it the fuck right up. 'No you do not!' I cuts it dead. Swipes the air to emphasise my point. 'What have I told you about that? ... You leave the thinking to me.'

It starts to nod, holds the plate against its chest and looks bashful. 'I'm sorry.'

I lets it go, because I'm just all fucking heart me. 'And see tomorrow, you can leave all the thinking to me as well ...'

It nods at me but it puts on that petted lip, the face like it's about to stamp its foot and say, 'But I never did anything!'

I sees I need to labour the point. 'You know all you have to do: take the last cash bag of the week out the safe at the end of the night — after you've cashed up all the bars, like — and then head out to the bar with your handbag for the end-of-the-night drink as usual ...' I cuts myself short, realises I should be testing it to make sure. 'And then what?'

It's shivering as it speaks. Daft cow's still in its wet clothes. 'Then I make my excuses to go to the ladies room ...'

'Uh-huh,' I nods away.

'When it is, how you say again, a clear coast.'

'I rolls my eyes, 'When the coast is clear ... Jesus, don't be getting hung up on the wording, when there's no cunt about right!'

'Yes. When the coast is clear, I pass the money through the window to you and then we go to Paris.'

I can feel my tongue pressing the inside of my mouth again and I wonder if that's the old nerves kicking in already. I feel like I'm about to lose the rag here. I mean, if Davie Geddes clocks it, then Monique can say goodbye to those good looks at the very least. Maybe more than that. 'Listen, Paris is a whole other stage away ... when I get the money through the window, what did I tell you happens next?'

'Ah yes.' It starts to smile, all pure chuffed with itself so it is. 'The rendezvous!'

'The what? ... I've told you to speak English for fucksake.'

It nods, all smiles. 'I leave for home, like I always do. I take a taxi cab, like I always do. And then we meet up at the flat and collect the rest of the money and our things for the journey.'

I gives it a reluctant nod. 'That's right. And then we go to Paris.'

*****

I can't say I find this usual, the nerves. It's just not like the Stauner at all to be twitching away like some kind of epi-wotsit. I've got the muscle in the cheek twitching and there's another one at the same caper in my jawline. Then there's the thing with the tongue pressing away at the usual spot inside my mouth; it's so red and sore after these last few days that I can actually taste a wee bit of blood there. This is not good. Not right. And not proper.

The only time I can remember the nerves playing up – apart from the Old Firm games, and that's understandable because there's nothing normal about thinking the Fenian bastards might take a win – is when my Old Boy got put away. I hate the thought coming into my head. I can see the dirty wee hoor's face like it was in the papers. I hated that time, when all the lads at the school were saying that

Peterhead was where they put every stoat–the-ball and that my Old Boy was one of them. I got into some fights then, but you have to take a stand; there's no way I was having that wee hoor giving my Old Boy a bad name just because it changed its mind after leading him on. The facts of life, likes.

I looks about the flat. There's nothing much here that I'll miss. There's the telly, but it's just a wee one. Piece of shite, really, I'm thinking. Monique's gear is all packed up and its two suitcases are piled at the door. Pink suitcases, by the way; I'm sure I'll not be lugging any pink fucking suitcase down to the street; not having anyone thinking I've gone and turned into a buftie boy. No way José; Monique can heft that down to the hire car herself.

I shoves a few wee items into my Gers bag, one with the red, white and blue handles, and I plant it on top of the pink eyesores. I gives it a wee pat and smiles, because I know that inside is the money that the bold Stauner has taken off Davie Geddes.

'Aye, you'll be laughing on the other side of your face when you go to check that bank vault on Monday, Davie,' I goes. I'm still smiling, even has a wee bit of a laugh to myself, because there's something to be said for getting one up on a bastard like that. I mean, all I was doing was dealing a bit of gear in his manky old club for fucksake and the reaction I got from him was well over the top.

For a moment I feel the twitch in my cheek accelerate as I remember Davie's reaction that night. He gave me a good doing over, but if he found out about this before I shoot the crow, then I'd be dead meat. 'Nah, he's more likely to take that razor to you,' I hears a voice inside my head yell at me.

I steps back because the voice is so real it makes me look over my shoulder to see if there is somebody there in the flat with me.

'Fucksake!' I goes as I realise I've let my imagination run away with me. 'Davie'll not get the chance to bring that razor within a mile of me, fucking sure he won't!'

I know I'll be on the motorway, heading to London, and then it's off to Paris and the new life on the nice bit of green I've got now. I gets a wee bit apprehensive thinking about the move, I mean, I don't know a soul in Paris — or the whole of France, even — but that's what I've got this daft lassie for. I reckons the best part of a month to get the lay of the land and then I'll be able to ditch it. I mean, with all that folding material in my possession and with the rep those French lassies have. I'll not be sticking to the one hole. No, sir, sure I won't. Be like sitting down to the same dinner every night of the week and I'm not for that. Monique will be getting the jotters sometime round about the third or fourth week, I reckon, and it can fucking whistle if it thinks I'll be handing over any of this poppy either.

'The fucking chancing cunt,' I goes.

I parks it back on the sofa and sparks up a Club kingsize. I'm down to my last pack of ten and I'm not best pleased about that fact at all. It's another one of those things that I have to add to the list about Monique: it's a lazy fucking cow when it comes to getting the shopping in.

'It knew I'd be gantin on a fag tonight, as well.'

I finds myself blasting it for all sorts and I'm even wondering if I'll manage to last the three or four weeks in Paris with it, but it comes into my head that I'll be scoobied without it speaking the lingo, so I lets the issue with the fags go and feels altogether better about it; I mean, you could never let it be said that the Stauner is an inconsiderate cunt, because there's some blokes would have it bounced off the four walls for a thing like forgetting to keep the fags well stocked.

Before I know it I've sat through an episode of Q.I. with that toffee-nosed buftie and I'm wondering how he gets away with it. Then I remembers that he's a queer and they've not got that handle for nothing. I've tanned the ten Club before I know it, but I'm cool with that because as I look at the clock I see it's time to rock and roll.

I picks up my Ben Sherman and leaves the zipper halfway down, just enough to show the wee Blues badge on the polo shirt. I takes a deck at myself in the mirror and I'm surprised to see the hair is wilting a wee bit, so I runs the fingers through with a bit of Dax on the tips and soon I'm back to form.

'Best-looking in the toon,' I goes.

In the street I seek out the hire car – a poxy wee Punto, not befitting of a man of my calibre, it has to be said, but then anything else would just be drawing attention to myself and I get enough of that from fifty per cent of the population as it is.

The roads are quiet after the wee bit of rain and with it being so late on, and as I pull onto Glasford Street I hears the mobi ping.

It's a text from Monique.

JUST ABOUT TO CASH UP HERE XX

I curls my lip at the kisses. I mean, what's it playing at there, eh? But I starts the countdown, because I needs to get back to business right away. If it's at the cashing-up then I have about fifteen-twenty minutes to get in place. I lifts my hands off the wheel and rubs them together. 'Soon be in the money, Stauner ... Not long now, my son.'

As I passes the Boneyard I spots a couple of big cunts out the front – two of Davie Geddes's pugs. One of them has an angry looking Mars Bar down the side of his coupon and it puts my nerves back on edge. Fair puts a dampener on the occasion, as I wonder to myself where he got that and if it was off the end of Davie's razor. Still, I drives on by and parks up, tries to get my mind on the task at hand. As I leaves the Punto and walks past the fire escape at the side of the club I hears the mobi ping again.

Heading for the bathroom.

I feels my heart kick. My blood starts to race and there's a big smile spreads right across my face.

'You dancer,' I goes, under my breath likes, because I'm trying to keep quiet as I squeeze past the empty barrels and get to the window.

I sees the lights beyond the windows, but I don't know which one is for the lassies' toilets. One of the windows is bigger than the other and I spot a few red and green lights flashing there, so I quickly suss that it's the window for the corridor to the club. I do a quick scan of the outside of the building to get my bearings and can see the gents' toilet is round the corner, so can pinpoint the lassies' toilet no bother.

'Bingo!' I goes. 'Right, Monique, just you lob that

bag of money down to Stauner and let's get this fucking show on the road.'

I waits for a couple of minutes in the freezing cold before I see a hand pressed on the windowpane. The glass is frosted and I can't see what's going on beyond but I somehow makes out that there's a problem.

'The fuck's going on?' I thinks to myself.

Suddenly the mobi pings again.

I CANNOT OPEN THE WINDOW

I can't believe this. I mean, for fucksake, did it never even check this out?

I texts it back.

WHAT DO YOU MEAN? IS IT LOCKED?

It replies.

THERE IS NO LOCK. IT DOES NOT OPEN AT ALL

I shakes my head. I am fully raging now. I can feel my hand clenching on the mobi.

WELL FUCKING BREAK IT

There's a long pause before it replies.

I CANNOT THERE IS NOTHING HERE TO BREAK IT

I takes a sketch about the wee alley at the side of the Boneyard and I finds fuck all. I start to panic because I'm wondering if Davie Geddes will be looking for Monique if it stays in the pisser for much longer. I can see the whole venture going tits up – Monique getting cut up – and for the first time the prospect of failure enters my head. I know it's panic and I quickly try to push the thought away, but for some reason I feel like the game has changed. A queasy feeling in the pit of my stomach has set up lodging and no matter how hard I try I can't get rid of it.

I look up at the dark night sky and I swear the fat cunt of a man in the moon is winking at me like he knows something I don't. I flick him the finger and run from the wee lane towards the car. I think about grabbing the tyre-jack and getting back in time, but then I think about the gig going wrong again. When I get back to the car I feel my heart freeze and I stop dead in my tracks.

'Alright, Stauner,' goes Tambo – Davie's top boy from the Boneyard is out front having a smoke with another pug.

'Yeah, not bad,' I goes.

The fat prick is sitting on the wall beside the Punto with a fag stuck in his grille; he's chatting to another no-neck roaster who's likely been stabbing himself in the arse with steroids since Adam was a boy. The pair look me up and down and then Tambo speaks again. 'You better not be thinking about setting foot inside that fucking club, lad.' He gets up off the wall and blows smoke in my eyes. As he does so, his mate stands behind me and places a fat mitt on my collar.

'No, I was just, er, passing by, Tam.' At once I regret these words.

The pair start to laugh and I feel my spine turn to jelly at the thought of everything going to shit in the next instant.

*****

'Are you taking the fucking piss?' goes the fat biffer with his hand on my collar.

'No. Do I look fucking thick?' I knows at once he can't give a smart-arse reply to that question because I'm looking the part in Ben Sherman and a proper quality Gers polo – not to mention the hair. He'd make himself out to be a right dick if he slapped down a man in my kit.

'Yeah,' he goes. 'You fucking do.'

I have to shake my head at this because he's clearly blind to the facts, but something – the queasy feeling in my gut, likely – stops me in my tracks and I double up and spew on the tarmac.

'Oh for fucksake,' goes Tambo. 'That's my good shoes!'

I utters an apology and leans on the side of the Punto. I feel my guts heave again and I puke once more. I see the pair watching me out the corner of my eye, but no one likes the smell of barf and Tambo starts to lead his mate away, looking back and jerking hand gestures at me.

'I'm gonna do you one of these days, Stauner,' goes Tambo. 'Just for the fucking hell of it.'

I know he means it as well.

When I've shed my guts I opens up the boot and grabs the jack. I hides it under my jacket and heads back to the wee lane at the side of the Boneyard. As I get back in position I'm poleaxed to see the lights are now out in the lassies' toilet.

'The fuck is going on?' I goes.

I takes out the mobi and there's no message from Monique, so I gets my own off.

WHERE HAVE YOU GONE?

I have to wait for an age to get a reply.

I'M BACK BEHIND THE BAR

I just can't believe what I'm seeing here. I get so angry I lash out and smack my knuckles off one of the empty barrels — it starts to topple and it's made a loud clatter off the ground before I can do a thing. I watch it roll towards the others and it sets a security light off. The light floods the wee lane and that's when I notice there's a CCTV camera on the side of the building.

'Fuck. Fuck. Fuck.'

I pins myself to the wall and starts to key into my mobi.

GET BACK TO THE TOILET WITH THE MONEY

It replies quickly this time.

I CANNOT. THE TOILET FLOODED. IT HAS BEEN CLOSED

I seriously can't get my head around it. I weigh my options up and they all look slim to none. I mean, I can hardly go in there and take the money off it — apart from the fact that someone might notice it handing me the cash bag, I'd have to get past the door pugs first.

'This isn't happening,' I tells myself.

I'm still pinned to the wall trying to avoid the security camera when my mobi pings.

GO TO THE DISABLED TOILET NEXT TO THE GENTS. I WILL BE THERE IN A MINUTE

I reads the message and tries to take it in. I quickly suss that they've obviously let the lassies use the disabled toilet whilst theirs is flooded out. Thing is, it's next to the gents' — which is round the corner, past the security camera.

'Oh, no!' I goes.

The only way past the camera is to pull my jacket up over my head, and I pass that option up right away because it will mess my hair up, so I hoists the jack above my head and pray that it obscures enough of my coupon to keep Davie Geddes from identifying me.

When I get round to the disabled toilet the light is on, but I hold off on smashing the window. I send a text.

ARE YOU THERE YET?

In a few minutes the light goes on and off and then a hand is tapped on the window.

YES HERE

I see it's Monique standing there at the window so I wait for it to move and then I throw the jack up. As I jumps out the way, expecting to see a shower of glass, the jack comes bouncing back and lands on the ground with a clatter. When I look up to check the damage to the window I see that it's toughened safety glass with the wee wire squares running through it like they used to have at the school.

'Fucking no way.'

I know this glass of old, and I know the only way to smash it is to shatter the lot and pull the wire out. I picks up the jack again and aims it at the top of the glass; I gets out the way as it bounces back. It takes another three or four attempts before I can get my hand onto the wire and then I yank it down towards the ground. In the panic, I've given up trying to dodge the CCTV camera, but my mind is on getting to the car and getting away as quickly as I can. I'm thinking, if we get rumbled on the job, Monique can fuckingwell fend for herself because I'll be Harry the Toff.

There's enough of a hole in the corner of the window now to feed the money through, but the cash bag jams there when Monique starts to pass it out.

'Push it ... push the fucker,' I tells it.

'It is stuck ...'

'Just push it.'

'I am pushing. I will need to remove the money.'

I shakes my head at this, but then I see the rolls of cash falling on the tarmac and I drops to pick them up. I can feel the adrenalin rushing through me as I hear Monique calling from the window in that wee Frenchie voice of hers, 'That is it all, darling ... do you have it?'

I'm too busy picking the rolls up and stuffing them into the pockets of my Ben Sherman to answer.

'Darling, I have to go back to the bar now.'

I hears it, but I'm fully in a trance now, scooping up the green bundles. There's more money than I imagined, thousands and thousands. My heart starts to flutter at the sight of it, and then it begins to race as I'm off, chanking it down the wee lane, feet thumping on the tarmac all the way towards the Punto. Geddes could be outside the toilet waiting for Monique with a razor in his mitt and I wouldn't give two fucks.

*****

The car starts in a oner and I'm heavy on the accelerator as I spin the wheels out of the car park. The first few streets are a blur of lights and bodies on the pavements as I try to keep the wheel from slipping through my sweaty palms. My mouth's as dry as a pie as I put the pedal to the metal and try to remember how to drive. I'm guffawing like a clown but I don't care. I've done it: I've taken Davie Geddes to the cleaners.

'Nice one, Stauner,' I tells myself as I clip the edge of the kerb in an overly ambitious tilt at a tight corner. 'Ooh, watch the wheels.'

I'm still laughing and yakking to myself — there's

folk would say I've lost it – but I don't care. I've done it. I've fuckingwell done it.

'Result, old son ... result!'

When I get into the street I drop the pace and start to trawl for a parking place. As usual the whole street's chocka with all the pishy motors the roasters drive down this way. I'm thinking about buying a decent car now that I'm fully wedged up – a wee 911 or something – I knows there's not a bint in the land would fail to perform if I had a Porsche.

'Y'fucking dancer, Stauner! You're in a different league now.'

I sees a wee space behind a crappy old Metro that's dripping in rust. I clips the front wing as I reverses in, but like I give a shite. The Punto will be abandoned down in the Smoke soon and I'll be on a fast-train to Paris with a bagful of moolah. My heart is still bucking like a brass on double-time when I slams the door and runs up to the flat. I have my arms round the rolls of cash inside my Ben Sherman and it's a comfort to know the Stauner is a man of means – self-made as well.

Inside the flat I grab the wee Gers bag with the red, white and blue handles and I unzip the top. I feels like a lottery-winner as I spy the bundles of green in there and when I open up my jacket front and tip in the latest haul I can hardly believe my eyes.

'Holy shit!'

There's so much cash I'm wondering will I even be able to close the bag. I picks the handles up and places the bag on the coffee table in the centre of the room and steps back. I look at the load, fivers, tenners and twenties all spilling over the top. I shakes my head and has to give a wee slap on the side of my face to see if I'm not dreaming.

'It's real alright, and it's all mine.'

I takes a step away and stares on with my hands on my hips. 'Aye, it's all mine.' I'm still staring when I hears a key in the door and I takes a jolt to myself.

Monique isn't expected back till later — after it's pretended to bank the takings and locked up the club for Geddes.

I stares on at the door to the living-room, waiting.

I hears footsteps. Not just one set either.

There's the sound of more movement.

I feels panic leap inside me; fear enters the room when I clock the first face to appear.

'You ...' I goes. My voice sounds unnatural, low as a child's as I take in the full view of Jonesy.

'Oh yes, Stauner.'

'But ...' I watch two more men come in behind him. At first I don't recognise them, though they seem familiar, then I remember where I've seen them before. 'I sold you pair some downers ... the night I was raided!'

They look at each other and smile. One pinches his nose and stifles a laugh. They don't look like druggie beat boys now.

'These boys are, er, friends of mine,' goes Jonesy.

'But ... I don't ...' I'm scoobied, can't seem to get a handle on things.

Jonesy steps forward and places a hand on my shoulder. 'Perhaps you should sit down, Stauner.' He nods to the other pair. 'Give him a fag, lads, think it's tradition and all that ... for the condemned man, likes.'

The lads start to laugh and one produces a pack of Benson's whilst the other leans over and sparks up a Bic lighter. I take the fag and draw the tobacco deep into my lungs; I notice my hands are shaking furiously now.

'Oh, and, just to avoid any doubt, Stauner ...' Jonesy leans over and picks up the Gers bag by its red, white and blue handles. 'I'll be relieving you of this.'

I tries to stand up, to object, but I get pushed back onto the sofa by the two boys, who seem much bigger and stronger than I remember. 'Hey that's my fucking money, that is!'

'Is that right now, Stauner?' goes Jonesy. 'I think you'll find it's actually mine.'

He starts to laugh and his pals join in. I seizes my

moment and dives out my seat, reaches for the bag. Jonesy steps to the side. It's a dummy the late Davie Cooper would have been proud of, and then I feel a kick to my gut and I roll towards the carpet. There's a spool of spit already unravelling from my mouth as I land.

Jonesy leans over me as I start to feel the sharpness of the pain working in my guts. 'That wasn't very smart, Stauner. But then you never were a very smart young man.' He kneels down beside me, takes my cheeks in his hand and squeezes tightly. He starts to speak through his bottom row of teeth as I begin to gag on my own stomach acid. 'No, always a bit of a daft cunt, weren't you? Always fancied yourself, that's what they used to say. If you were chocolate, you'd eat yourself ...'

I can hear the other two laughing at me. Out of the edge of my vision I can see them moving around the room. They pick up Monique's pink suitcases and I wonder what they plan to do with a pile of French knickers and little black dresses.

'Aye, fancying your chances was your downfall, Stauner. That and being too fucking stupid to realise that you weren't the dog's bollocks you thought you were. But, you know what, a lot of daft bastards go around with your delusions ... do you know what your big problem was?' He squeezes my face harder. I feel the bile in my gut rise. A little of the foul-tasting liquid enters my mouth. I try to open my mouth, but Jonesy has it clamped shut as he goes on.

'Your number one failing, Stauner, was inflicting your stupidity on others. You made a big mistake when you thought you could get away with poking my wee sister ... did you really think I was going to let you off with that? She was fourteen and she never got over it. You killed my wee sister.'

I want to tell him that his sister was a wee prick-teaser like all the rest of them, but I can't get the words out. I want to say they were all after it round the back of Tatty Tait's and Janie was no different. I want to yell this at him, but the words are trapped inside me.

'Did you think I'd let you just do a wee bit of time like your stoat-the-ball father?' He starts to rap my head off the floor. It's like he's emphasising his point now: each thud of skull on floor a reminder he has a point to make and he doesn't want me to forget it. 'No chance! They let him out and he was back at it ... makes you wonder where you got your ideas from, doesn't it?'

I can see the others back from loading the car. They stand behind Jonesy and fold their hands in front of their coat fronts. When Jonesy realises they're behind him he releases his grip and I gasp for air, choking and writhing on the carpet as I puke and spew all over the place. I think there's more to come from Jonesy, like he's been storing it up all these years and there must be more to follow but he says nothing, merely walks from the room and leaves the others to finish up.

'Get his arms,' goes one of them.

'Why? Pointless tying him up if we're going to knock him out,' goes the other.

I turn to see what they're doing and that's when I see the long needle. It's not the kind you usually see doctors with, or in a hospital even.

'What the fuck's that?' I goes.

The taller of the two bends down and punches me in the face. I feel my head spin and I slink back. The lights on the ceiling start to go in and out of focus.

'Get his trousers off.'

'Get the fuck off me ...' I goes.

'It's going in his arse, isn't it ...?'

Another punch on the head and then my eyes close and I go all woozy. I feel my trousers being removed and then I feel a sharp pain in my arsecheek.

'Look at the fucking state of that,' goes one of the pair standing over me. I'm too weak and addled to know which.

'And Monique was fucking him?'

'For a few weeks, as well ...'

'She'll be desperate for a good shag now.'

The pair laugh. Their voices echo off the walls as I fall in and out of a deep sleep, which I try to fight, but in the end I know it's useless to resist.

*****

I wake with my face pressed down on something hard. There feels like a weight on my back that's forcing my chest down and constricting my lungs. I can barely breathe, but every time I do manage to grasp some air I get a shooting jet of pain right in my arsehole.

'Oh, Jesus ...' I try to raise my face from the floor but the movement brings more shooting pain down my back and arse.

I start to slowly regain my senses and the first one is smell.

'Shit ...' I smell shit. And piss.

I press down on my palms and manage to raise my head and open my eyes.

'Oh, no ...' I'm lying in a pool of my own piss. I seem to have shit myself as well, and there's blood too – all down my bare legs.

I drag myself up a little more, manage to shift the weight — which is a broken barstool — from my back. As I raise myself onto my knees I feel an urge to run my hands down my back, towards my arse. When I reach the base of my spine I feel my fingers tremble — I sense something isn't right — but I force myself to reach further, beyond my hips and then — suddenly — I jerk back.

'Oh, God, no ...'

I twist my neck, manage to get my vision aligned just enough to see that there is a broken broom handle sticking out of my arse. It's been snapped in two and at its base I can see the streaks of blood where it's been shoved inside me. I try to grip it, to pull it out, but the pain is too much. I feel like passing out.

'Stauner, y'prick ...' I hear the words, but there's no one there. 'Aye, you, y'daft bastard.'

It's Tambo. I'd know that voice anywhere. As I widen my eyes and look about, all I see is the bright lights and that's when I realise I'm in the middle of a dance floor.

'Aye, Stauner, you're not wrong. Tambo is here – I'd pay for front-row seats to see this.' He starts to laugh and his voice bounces all around me.

From somewhere I get the strength to rise to my feet, I grip tight on the broom handle, fuelled more by shame than anything else, and I twist it. The pain shoots through my insides, but I feel the tip of the handle moving. I yell out in agony as the wood tears at my arse on the way out.

I hold the piece of wood for a second or two and then I let it fall. As I stand there a stream of warm blood starts to pour from my arsehole. 'This can't be happening ...'

'Oh aye it is, Stauner ... fucking sure it is.'

I feel a deep fear welling inside me. 'Tambo?' I go. 'That you? ... Show yourself ...'

The laughter kicks up again. But he remains in the shadows. I feel my full senses kick in now, and I realise I'm in the Boneyard. I'm in Davie Geddes's club, but I've no idea how I got here. I run a hand up to touch my hair and get the shock of my life to discover it's gone.

'Oh, Jesus, no ...' I look at the dance floor. There's hair everywhere, on me, on the floor. *My* hair, but the lassies love my hair.

I can't take it. I starts to weep. 'Help me!'

As I call out, I hear laughter.

'Tambo, that you? What the fuck have I ever done to you?'

More laughs.

Mad laughs.

A door slams.

Through the darkness I hear something else.

Footsteps.

Slow, at first.

Then faster.

There's a kerfuffle. A shuffle of bodies and raised

voices.

'No. No. No.' I don't want to know what comes next.

Suddenly the lights are turned up, right up, into eye-burning brightness. I see my bare legs. My bare feet. And the scattering of empty cash bags and altered receipts on the floor. I tug at the edges of my shirttails and try to cover my cock and balls, but the light is too strong for me and I have to release a hand to shade my eyes. I start to shiver and there's the recollection of what has happened. I see images of Monique, of the money, and of Jonesy. They all flash before me and blend with the blinding light.

Everything feels unreal – I don't know what reality is anymore. I feel blood running from my arse down the back of my legs and I feel the hair that has been cut from my head under my bare feet. I feel stupidly young and lost, but not alone.

I hear all the voices echoing off the dance floor and the walls of the Boneyard and that's when I remember wee Janie Jones and the night round the back of the shop on the crates. Janie's dead now, that's what wee Ally had told me in the bookies. I wonder why I'm thinking about that, but it seems to be the most important fact of my whole life now.

'You ...' Davie Geddes's voice, loud and firm and full of rage, booms at me.

'Davie, I need to explain.'

He walks down the steps at the edge of the dance floor. As he comes into view I see his pyjama collar under his overcoat. His head shakes, his eyes burn. 'You ...'

'Davie, please ...' I see the open razor in his hand, the kind they call a cut-throat, and I panic. 'It was the lassie ... the French lassie set me up, Davie. It was all a trap.'

'Save yourself the bother because there's no words on this earth are going to make an ounce of difference to me here and now.'

I feel my knees go as he speaks. I drop and a loud crack of bone on wood rattles round the club. I feel eyes on me, eyes and breath. I know there's others here in the Boneyard but the bright lights hide their faces. As I kneel down I feel a hand on the roof of my skull and my head is tipped back violently.

Davie Geddes speaks quietly – to me alone: 'You get to my age, see the things I've seen, and you think there's nothing else to see.'

'Davie, please ...'

'And then something comes along and it makes you think, really, you've seen nothing ... nothing at all. That bit of film they just showed me, with you smashing up my back window – I couldn't believe my eyes. I couldn't believe anyone would have balls big enough for that, or be so fucking stupid.'

'Davie, I'm begging you ... I'll get your money back. I promise, I'll get all the money ...'

He places a hand over his lips, motions me to be silent. 'Oh, this goes way beyond the money now. This goes well and truly beyond the realms of taking money from Davie Geddes.' He lowers his hand, places it on my head and tilts my neck further towards the edges of the dance floor. I sense the eyes on me again and I swear I can feel the stillness of all eternity.

'You see this,' roars Davie to everyone watching, 'you see this and you go tell people what happens when you try to fuck Davie Geddes up the arse!'

He lunges back quickly and hoists the razor as high as he can reach.

It feels like a punch in the neck when the steel slices into me.

The high arc of bright-red blood lands a long way across the floor and my heart pumps more of the same to follow it.

Where I lie, I know that's it for the Stauner.

I know there's no more to come.

The facts of life, likes.

Another story you may like to try

THE HOLY FATHER by Tony Black

When young Scots carpenter Joe is visited by the Wing Wizard Davie Cooper one Christmas Eve he gets the shock of his life — his partner is to give birth to a king that very night. Setting off through their scheme — guided only by an unusual, yet familiar, constellation — Joe and Mary-doll soon discover their shared passion for the opposing ends of the Scottish football terraces unites them in ways they could never have imagined. *The Holy Father* is a 7,000 word short story delving into the divisive nature of Scottish football, told in the raw Scots tongue, and delivered in a familiar festive setting.

About the Author

Tony Black is an award-winning journalist and the author of some of the most critically acclaimed British crime fiction of recent times. His Gus Dury series features: *Paying for It, Gutted, Loss* and *Long Time Dead*, which is soon to be filmed for the big screen by Richard Jobson. A police series featuring DI Rob Brennan includes: *Truth Lies Bleeding* and *Murder Mile*. He is also the author of the recently published *Artefacts of the Dead (2014)* and the novellas *The Storm Without*, *The Inglorious Dead, R.I.P. Robbie Silva, Long Way Down, Last Orders* and *The Ringer*. His first novel outside the crime genre, *His Father's Son* was followed up by *The Last Tiger* in 2014.

Visit his website at: **www.tonyblack.net**

Printed in Great Britain
by Amazon